START HERE:
Volume II

Read Your Way Into 25 Amazing
Authors

Edited by Jeff O'Neal & Rebecca Joines Schinsky

Riot New Media Group, Inc. | *New York, 2013*

ISBN: 978-1-6192773-4-2

Book Riot, Inc
bookriot@bookriot.com
Brooklyn, NY
http://bookriot.com

ACKNOWLEDGEMENTS

Start Here, Volume II was launched through Kickstarter.com. We are grateful to all 1233 people who backed the project, including the following people who loved the project enough to go above and beyond.

Alexandria Masud, Angelica Nohemi Quinonez, Ann Ingram, Janet Berkman, Jeff Seymour, Joanne Kelly, JR Hughson, Kim Borgmeyer, Mandy Boles, Melissa Aho, Neely Tucker, Nicola F. Biasi, Sarah Burnes, Shelly Nuessle, Sushil K Gupta, and The NYC Casselonnollies.

TABLE OF CONTENTS

INTRODUCTION

by Jeff O'Neal

The best way, by far, to find something to read is to get a recommendation from someone you know. You can tell them your preferences, get a sense of their taste, and ask questions. The trouble is, you probably don't know someone who can give you a recommendation for all of the authors you're interested in; you can only get recommendations about books and authors they've read.

So while you don't know us, here's who we are — a bunch of passionate readers who want you to try the authors you've always wanted to try but haven't known how to get started. Each of these chapters was written by someone who loves the author's work and knows it inside and out. We know their strengths and we know their weaknesses. We know what we love about them and what others will love about them. There are authors, and PhDs, and critics writing here, but first and foremost we are readers writing for other readers.

Start Here is a field guide. It is not meant to be definitive or exhaustive. We imagine you taking it with you to the bookstore and thumbing through it as you decide if you'd like to try Dickens or Atwood or Melville for the first time. Perhaps you'll pull it up on your ereader before pouring that Sunday morning coffee and downloading a book. And, after spending a few minutes reading a chapter, we hope you'll feel excited and confident about picking something new.

We don't want to tell you what to think or why to think it. We want you to take what we know and love about these authors and figure out how to know and love them for yourself. Because that's the important thing — adding books to your life that make it deeper and fuller.

All of these authors can do that. Time to get started.

ISAAC ASIMOV

by Peter Damien

My real education, the superstructure, the details, the true architecture, I got out of the public library. For an impoverished child whose family could not afford to buy books, the library was the open door to wonder and achievement, and I can never be sufficiently grateful that I had the wit to charge through that door and make the most of it.

Isaac Asimov
I, Asimov: A Memoir

Isaac Asimov (b. 1920) was a wildly prolific American author, who wrote or edited more than 500 books. Best known for his science fiction writing, Asimov also wrote mystery, fantasy, non-fiction, and was a professor of biochemistry at Boston University.

On the face of it, Isaac Asimov doesn't seem like that difficult an author to get into. His prose was always straight-forward, simple, and readable. It was absolutely bare-bones, something he was unapologetic for, and that seems easy enough. It just gets intimidating when you zoom out a little and realize that he wrote **over 400 books**. True enough, there's some contention about how many books he actually wrote...but frankly, if your body of work is so huge as to generate contention, then it doesn't matter how many books are in it. It's big.

1. *The Caves of Steel* (1954)

Now you might be looking at that choice a little oddly and wondering why not **I, Robot**, which is the first robot book? Why the second? Simple. **I, Robot**, while a very groundbreaking and brilliant book, is a collection of disjointed stories that might put off a reader in ways that the unified story of a novel won't.

What *Caves of Steel* has going for it is that it offers a whodunit detective story, a genre that Asimov loved as dearly as science fiction. It's a book that brims with enthusiasm and love and fun, and it's exciting to shoot through it. It's as fun as watching a Columbo murder-mystery movie...except this has robots in it. Robots improve everything. That's just a fact. The story presents us with Elijah Baley, a detective from the overcrowded New York of the future, an Earth where people are so used to being packed in and living their lives in tiny apartments and hallways, the mere hint of a stretch of land is enough to cause panic attacks. Elijah Baley is one of Asimov's strongest characters, and not least because of his relationship with his partner, R. Daneel Olivaw. R stands for Robot. They are, in my opinion, one of the finest and most enjoyable detective duos you can find in books, and it's a pleasure to revisit them.

Reading *The Caves of Steel* will provide you with the small amount of acclimation you might need to read Asimov. That taken care of, we can head on...

2. *Foundation* (1951)

From there, we head into the major leagues with what might be Asimov's science fiction novel stuffed with his biggest and most ambitious ideas. Hari Seldon and his group of psychohistorians have figured out mathematically that the great and timeless Galactic Empire is crumbling and will collapse over the next few centuries. To deal with what he sees as the certainty of approaching chaos and barbarism, Seldon proposes that a Foundation be set up, deep in space, populated with all of the greatest minds the Empire can provide. They will follow their own intellect and Seldon's grand and mysterious plan to ensure that over the course of hundreds and hundreds of years, the collapse and reconstruction of the Empire proceed exactly on a schedule.

The book skips generations, visiting successive generations of the Foundation and its leaders in a series of what are essentially short stories. The changes don't feel particularly abrupt, because while Asimov's style might be plain, he was always a very gifted writer and the characters welcome you instantly into each story. There's a great many ideas bubbling around in the book beyond the simple plot-ideas of the collapse of an Empire and the birth of a Foundation. There are moral questions about what it means to allow the Empire to collapse, what it means to remain technologically superior--but also morally superior--to the primitive cultures that grow up around you. Many of the questions surrounding Hari Seldon and whether or not anyone should listen to his Master Plan wander into almost theological territory...but never so heavily that you feel as if you're reading a tedious allegory. The stories come at you light and fast and easy, but they leave an awful lot behind when you're done.

3. *Fantastic Voyage II: Destination Brain* (1987)

Something we forget about Asimov is that he wrote a lot of books that weren't about robots or Hari Seldon's Foundation, and I think it's important to take a look at those, because some of them were excellent. In the 1960s, Asimov was asked to write the novelization for a movie coming out called *Fantastic Voyage*, and he did it *so quickly* that the novelization came out well before the movie, causing some people to think it was a movie based on Asimov's novel. His novel, though, was done off of Harry Kleiner's screenplay, and that meant there were bits Asimov was unsatisfied with. So in 1987, Asimov published this book, *Fantastic Voyage II*, and I've chosen this sequel rather than the original, because the ideas in here are all Asimov's.

The original idea is classic: a team of scientists are shrunk down to molecule size and inserted into a person's body in a special submarine (you know, like in *Innerspace* with Martin Short). In *Destination Brain*, a team again goes into the body stuck in a coma, this time heading for the brain. Obviously. It's a rollicking adventure with some excellent science along the way.

———————————————

From these three books, you've got a good handle on Asimov. Not only his major series and themes, but also his writing style from various points in his writing career, although frankly it changed very little. From here, you can wander freely through his massive bibliography, through the long Robot and Foundation series, and maybe even into his nonfiction.

You can thank me when you're done reading all his books, but it may be a few years.

OCTAVIA E. BUTLER

by Cassandra Neace

If you want a thing--truly want it, want it so badly that you need it as you need air to breathe, then unless you die, you will have it. Why not? It has you. There is no escape. What a cruel and terrible thing escape would be if escape were possible.

Octavia Butler
The Parable of the Talents

Octavia Butler (1947-2005) was a pioneer in the world of science fiction and fantasy. Her novels and short stories were best sellers. In addition to multiple Nebula, Locus, and Hugo awards, she was awarded a MacArthur Foundation "Genius" Grant in 1995.

At an event at Copperfield's Books, author Junot Diaz was asked who he would be if he could be any other author. His answer came as a surprise to many. He said that he would be Octavia Butler. She is, it seems, his idol. He was a kid who grew up reading SciFi. In college, he discovered literature by authors of color and was moved by the works of authors like Toni Morrison, Leslie Marmon Silko, and Oscar Hijuelos. With Octavia Butler, he could have it all.

Butler was something of a pioneer. She was an African American woman writing a genre that was dominated by white men. She not only found success in doing so, but she earned the recognition of her peers and the adoration of her readers. And she deserved it.

She first gained recognition with a group of novels known as the *Patternist* series. I would suggest that you start there, but since the novels were published out of chronological order, I don't think that she would expect us to read *any* of her books in order. I don't even think that we need to start with whole books. Instead, do as I did, and start with some of her award-winning short fiction.

"Speech Sounds" is a great story to start with for someone still new to the world of science fiction and fantasy. There's not too much of either. It's more a speculative fiction piece, one that considers what it would be like if we lost the ability to speak and/or to read and write. How would we communicate? How would we solve conflicts? How would we accomplish something as simple as taking the bus to Pasadena? It's got sex, violence, and hope – ingredients that every speculative fiction story should have. Or, at least that's what I've gleaned from reading Margaret Atwood.

From there, take a look at **"Blood Child."** The story takes place on a distant planet, one where humans arrived and found themselves at the mercy of the native species. They live their lives and raise their families while living in a preserve. They are protected, nurtured even. In exchange for this protection, the humans must make certain sacrifices. This story is about a young man who comes to understand just what that sacrifice entails. Butler writes in the afterword about how people think the story is about slavery, but that wasn't her intent. It was, she writes, inspired by botflies, colonialism, and curiosity about what it would be like for a man to be pregnant. It's a fascinating story.

Next, try her most popular novel, the one that enabled her to be a full-time writer – *Kindred* **(1979).** This time, Butler meant to write about slavery. A woman named Dana, living in the modern age, finds herself traveling back in time. The trips are unexpected and unpredictable. Initially, she does not realize that it is her own history that she is stepping in to. She meets her ancestors and becomes a part of their story. Butler never explains how Dana makes these trips or what enables them. She leaves science completely out of it. Instead, she referred to this novel as a "grim fantasy," one that let people experience the psychological and emotional trauma that came with being a slave.

Science fiction and fantasy have a bad reputation in some circles. They are thought to have less depth than other types of fiction. The label "escapist" is applied liberally. Authors like Butler, however, prove that these criticisms are unfounded. Her work is incredibly profound. She may have chosen to take her readers to another place, another time, or another planet in the telling of her stories, but, in doing so, she makes them realize important truths about themselves and the world that are living in.

ANNE CARSON

by Loyal Miles

quid amor valeat nesciam

why love prevails I have no idea

Anne Carson
Nox

Anne Carson *(b. 1950) is a poet, essayist, and translator. Carson's books include translations of ancient Greek poetry and drama, verse novels, essays (sometimes in verse) on desire, gender, and the Bronte sisters, poetry, and imaginary television treatments of Hector, Tolstoy, and Lazarus (among others). Publishers list her bio as follows: "Anne Carson was born in Canada and teaches ancient Greek for a living." Her many honors include a MacArthur Fellowship (a genius grant). Carson's writing has been praised for its playfulness and ambition, its emotional daring and vast scholarship, and its urgency and inventiveness.*

I saw Anne Carson before I read her. It was a reading at a Brooklyn bookstore. In bright red running shoes and red barrettes, Carson spirited behind and around and in front of the podium. I'm not the first to say this, but that night I got the feeling she was just as likely to have emerged from the subway as to have dropped from the sky. Carson's work is strange. Even as she grounds her writing in the old questions—the what-is-the-essence-of-life questions that date back to the ancients—a straining for newness and otherness characterize Carson's books. That's part of what makes her writing so distinct: from the first word to the last, and usually in the absence of plot, Carson invites (and often *jolts*) readers out onto some intellectual or emotional limb, where there's no promise that language (English or ancient Greek or otherwise) will be capable of communicating the depth of whichever fundamental feature of human life—desire, love, death, family, identity etc.—Carson (and her readers with her) find themselves grappling.

Her books are not like other books. Consider *Nox*, a 2010 elegy for her brother, in which Carson presents a translation of a Roman elegy alongside a variety of verse and prose intermixed with scrapbook-like materials, including black and white photos of her brother and herself as children in rural Ontario. Many of these photos have an aged fade, a sepia tone in which the landscape and the Carson siblings stand beneath a white flash of sky that seems to glow with childhood long-ago and all the wonder and longing that pulse through the best of Carson's writing.

A few guideposts are helpful before starting into the books. First, most of Carson's work doesn't fit easily into one genre. As a March 2013 *New York Times Magazine* profile put it: "Carson is usually referred to as a poet, but just about no one finds that label satisfying: her fans (for whom she does something more than poetry), her critics (for whom she does something less than poetry) or herself." Such ambiguity is part of reading Carson. About *If Not, Winter*, a translation of more than 150 fragments of poems by Sappho, Carson said in *The Paris Review* in 2004,

> *The magic of fragments [is] the way that [each] poem breaks off leads into a thought that can't ever be apprehended. There is the space where a thought would be, but which you can't get hold of. I love that space . . . Nothing fully worked out could be so arresting, so spooky.*

Dealing with fragments and ideas you can't quite get hold of is part of the Carson experience, as are the following: an emphasis in her poems on plain language even in the context of scholarly-like references to ancient and/or other complicated texts, an occasional unevenness/stiltedness perhaps resulting from Carson's effort to make every sentence new, an often inexplicable approach to line breaks, and a consistent ability at the end of books to deliver a jarring, moving moment.

I can't imagine Carson would welcome an ordered guide to her work—she seems to want her readers to discover multiple entryways as they circle with her around and through an idea—but here's one reader's map, moving from an essay through two verse novels to *Nox*, which is like no other book I've ever read.

1. *Eros the Bittersweet* (1986)

Carson's first book is an exceptional lyric essay on desire, imagination, reading, and the will *to know*. The book also provides a very readable introduction to ancient Greek poetry and writing, as Carson describes ancient writers' takes on eros/desire (including the myth of King Midas and Socrates's moving case for risking desire). *Eros the Bittersweet* is Carson as teacher and guide. She insists that desire is a verb, an active reaching of the self toward what's desired—a movement through the space that separates lack or absence from presence. She explores the ancient Greek belief that this process is inherently dangerous. The presence we desire may not turn out to be what we've imagined. Even riskier, we are likely to find ourselves changed by the act of reaching for and taking hold of what we desire. Carson compares the eros-fueled straining of self toward something unknown to a similar reaching that occurs in reading (as we imagine our way into a space created by words, separate from the reality around us) and in knowing (as we ask questions and reach for answers that may—and if the questions are important, that must—change our lives).

2. *The Beauty of the Husband: A Fictional Essay in 29 Tangos* (2001)

The back cover describes this book as "an essay on Keats's idea that beauty is truth [and] the story of a marriage." A quote from Keats begins each of the 29 sections, and like an essay the book concludes with reference notes (referenced texts include *Iliad*, *Jane Eyre*, and *History of the Peloponnesian War*). But we also have a wife and a husband in a marriage coming apart, and we have dialogue and setting and peripheral characters—not the stuff of essay. I would advise reading the book as poetry. Much of the writing is in verse, and even if the verse mostly feels like prose, the nature and effect of the book seems closest to the condensed intensity of poetry—situation and action remain a little nebulous and fragmented throughout while individual moments and scraps of language rise to the fore. One possible entry point is to read the wife as Truth and the wayward husband as Beauty, as Carson challenges Keats's idea that Beauty is Truth. But there is something deeper and very personal in the "story" of the separated

32

wife and husband, a gut-level sadness that had me leaning against my kitchen counter after finishing the book, and this ability to use language to create an experience of some mysterious and perhaps inarticulate truth is why so many identify Carson as a poet.

3. *Autobiography of Red: A Novel In Verse* (1998), with a few notes on *Red Doc>* (2013)

An imagined interview with a lesser-known ancient Greek poet who may have been blinded by Helen (yes, that Helen), the pre-story of the creatures (human and otherwise) at the center of one of Hercules's labors, adolescent love, growing up gay, living in the shadow of a volcano, feeling oneself to be a monster, actually being a monster—Carson works all this into *Autobiography of Red*, her most popular and commercially successful book. Framed by translations of and that imagined interview with ancient Greek poet Stesichoros, the book presents the coming-of-age story of Geryon, a boy who is also a winged red monster (with Carson one thing is almost always also something else).

This book made Carson famous. It was blurbed by no less than Alice Munro and Michael Ondaatje. The *New York Times Book Review* called it "a profound love story." I include all this because *Autobiography of Red* is not my favorite Carson. For me, a lightness of tone throughout much of the book conflicts with the nature of some of the content in a way that can feel arbitrary and unproductively unsettling (though I will say that as always Carson delivers a profoundly moving ending).

Fifteen years after *Autobiography of Red*, Carson published a sequel: *Red Doc>*. This book is also not my favorite Carson. Its best moments—and some of the best moments in all of Carson's work—are when she writes about family. The sections in *Red Doc>* about G's (the adult Geryon's) loss of his mother echo the end of *Men in the Off Hours* (2001), which closes with Carson's beautiful meditation on her mother's death. In this meditation, Carson frames her grief in part through a description of sections that Virginia Woolf crossed out in her journals and manuscripts. Under the veneer of this serious but quirky scholarship (the crossouts in Virginia Woolf's journals!), Carson confronts the deep sadness caused by the death of a loved one. The below excerpt from a Woolf manuscript which Carson includes near the end of *Men in the Off Hours* highlights Carson's effort to counterbalance the pain of living with amazement at all that a life can be:

> *such*
>
> *abandon   Obviously it is impossible, I thought , looking into those*
>
> *ment   foaming waters, to*
>
> *such   compare the living with the dead make any comparison*
>
> *rapture   compare them.*

4. *Nox* (2010)

Perhaps it is my appreciation for Carson's ability to write about family that makes *Nox* my favorite of her books. She began the book, an elegy for her brother, many years before its publication, a delay caused partly by the difficulty of publishing the book as Carson desired: a kind of scrapbook become art object. Sold only in hardcover, the book opens a bit like a suitcase with the pages inside all connected accordion-style. It's not something you can read in bed or on the train. *Nox* requires physical engagement, unfolding the paper, examining the black and white photos, handwritten letters, drawings, and scraps of paper. Much of the book is made to look scissor-cut, time-faded, creased and torn, and glued together. You're likely to find yourself running your fingers over the text and around the edges of photos.

This is another Carson book that is more than one thing. On the left-hand side of most pages, *Nox* is a word-by-word translation of a Latin elegy written by the Roman poet Catullus for his brother. On the right-hand side are the scrapbook objects and Carson's writing about her own brother, who ran away in the 1970s and never returned, across the decades a few scattered letters and calls from overseas all that Carson and her mother had to know his status and whereabouts. If you've read enough of Carson by the time you reach *Nox*, you know how much family means to her, how much it weighs on her, and here she's struggling to write about the loss of a brother who for many years was absent but still alive, whose death followed the death of Carson's mother, leaving her the last living member of her family.

Carson approaches the mystery of her brother's absence and presence in her life as a translation project, and the reader struggles with her as she tries to use the ancient words of a Roman elegy to construct some meaning from the life and death of her brother. Carson has said her aim was not to gain an understanding of death but instead to make "something beautiful" out of death's "ugly chaos." Perhaps then it is no surprise that the outside of *Nox*, with the exception of a small strip of a childhood photo of her brother, is gray and heavy and ugly. But that photo, edged by a thin strip of yellow, is a keyhole into what's inside: an experience circling around and through human connection and loss, through the fabric of language, through what's beyond understanding: that given all we know still we love.

DOUGLAS COUPLAND

by Brenna Clarke Gray

We speak in sentences that end before finishing. We sleep heavily because we need to ask so many questions as we dream alone. We bump into others and feel bashful at recognizing souls so similar to ourselves.

Douglas Coupland
Shampoo Planet

Douglas Coupland (b. 1961) is perhaps best known as the writer who popularized the terms "Generation X" and "McJob" in his first novel, Generation X: Tales for an Accelerated Culture, that made an enormous splash in 1991. Since then, Coupland has written many other books and spearheaded a range of of other projects, from designing a line of clothing for Roots to the National Firefighters Memorial in Ottawa, ON.

I've been working on Coupland's writing for a long time — embarrassingly, I once yelled "I have a PhD in you!" at him before being subdued by police (okay, the last part didn't happen) — and one thing I hear from people is that Coupland, like any prolific artist, can seem kind of intimidating to approach.

So maybe you haven't read a Coupland since 1991, or maybe you've seen a bunch of stuff about the new *Girlfriend in a Coma* pilot and you're wondering about the man behind the story. Here are my four must-read books for getting a good sense of who Coupland is and how he does his writerly thang.

1. *Hey Nostradamus!* (2003)

I almost always tell people to start with 2003's *Hey Nostradamus!* for a few reasons, aside from it being one of my favourite all-time reads. First, the story — about a suburban school shooting and its long-reaching aftermath — is really compelling, and the novel is a quick read because of that. Second, it's a good novel for showcasing Coupland's ability to carefully and thoughtfully build voice and character, as the novel has four different focalizers with really distinct identities. And finally, it's an excellent introduction to major Coupland themes like suburban life, faith, spiritual identity, loneliness, and catastrophe.

2. *Souvenir of Canada* and/or *Souvenir of Canada 2* (2002 and after).

Okay, American Lit critics and scholars. This is me throwing down the gauntlet. You all have to stop just absorbing Douglas Coupland into your canon because it's convenient to do so. To really understand Coupland, you have to understand how a kind of 1960s Canadian centennial nationalism really helped shape his identity and his reading of the world. *Souvenir of Canada* was a major multi-faceted art project involving books, a documentary, and multiple art installations in Canada and the UK. This touches on another key aspect of reading Coupland — the visual arts are such a prominent part of how Coupland thinks about the world that to leave any examination of them out of an examination of him is to miss a significant aspect. Coupland tags this project as a way to explain Canada to non-Canadians, so pick it up and learn a thing or two, eh?

3. JPod (2006)

In 2006, Coupland released what was called the spiritual sequel to 1995's *Microserfs*. Set in a Vancouver game design company, *JPod* is all about the aimless Generation Y slackers picking up where the Generation X folk left off. Most significant to a discussion of Coupland, though, is that Douglas Coupland is a character in this novel. An evil, evil character. A complete asshole of a character. Seeing how Coupland constructs his own writing process in his fictionalized doppelgänger is revealing, I think. And finally, because you looked at *Souvenir of Canada*, you have a good sense of Coupland's visual perspective and you'll be ready for the kind of play shown in this image from the text.

4. *Girlfriend in a Coma* (1998)

Okay, the culmination: one of Coupland's absolute finest pieces of writing. All that you've experienced so far — loneliness, visual thinking, anxiety, spirituality — is combined in a phenomenal apocalyptic vision of teenagehood suspended and life squandered. A pregnant teenager slips into a coma and, while waiting for her to emerge, the people around her fail to move on. But what happens with the apocalypse comes while they're waiting for life to find its own meaning? It's beautiful and evocative, sad and sweet, life-affirming and profoundly troubling. And I'm so jealous of anyone about to read it for the first time.

ROALD DAHL

by Rita Meade

I myself have always found it difficult to treat anything too seriously and I believe the world would be a better place if everyone followed my example. I am completely without ambition. My motto - 'It is better to incur a mild rebuke than to perform an onerous task' - should be well known to you by now. All I want out of life is to enjoy myself.

Roald Dahl
My Uncle Oswald

Roald Dahl was born on September 13, 1916 in South Wales and died November 23, 1990 in Oxford. He wrote 19 novels for children, dozens of short stories for adults, biographies, and received many awards for his fiction and work on television.

If you were like me, you read every single one of Roald Dahl's books that you could get your hands on as a kid. In fact, you read them multiple times. You had nightmares about well-dressed witches turning you into a mouse. You believed wholeheartedly in Oompa-Loompas and Vermicious Knids. You could wholeheartedly relate to Matilda's ferocious, life-consuming love of reading, even if you didn't know at the time that reading Dahl's books helped to foster this same love in yourself.

You also probably didn't know that Dahl was as prolific a writer for adults as he was for children. Thankfully, the Dahl adventures don't have to end just because you grew up. (Note: it is acknowledged that Roald Dahl was a controversial, flawed man who sometimes said and did bad things. Readers will need to decide for themselves if they can separate the man from the literature. In the spirit of the rest of the book, this chapter will focus mostly on the literature and only a little bit on the man – and the attitudes - behind it.)

I'll be discussing three of Dahl's short story collections and his sole full-length novel for adults. The goal of this suggested reading pathway is to give the reader a sense of Dahl's growth as a writer and also to move from stories that are more innocuous (as innocuous as Dahl can be, anyway) to stories that are more shocking and salacious. It's not an exhaustive list by any means, but it will give you a taste of "quintessential Dahl" and perhaps, for better or for worse, alter your childhood conception of his work.

First, start with...

1. *Someone Like You* (1953)

One of the strengths of Dahl's writing, in both his short stories and his books, is creating enormous tension in what appear to be the most ordinary of circumstances. Banal or commonplace events - dinnertime conversation between a husband and wife, a walk in the garden, even the birth of a baby - quickly turn into scenes of horror.

This particular collection eases in the uninitiated with short, intense stories that aren't TOO scandalous (relative to later ones), but that still pack a satisfying punch. The basic themes center around the dishonest parts of human nature and the price that people can pay for trying to scam, cheat, and otherwise bamboozle their fellow man. Each story contains some degree of irony and suspense - Dahl loved to employ a twist ending, and often surreptitiously foreshadowed them early on in the text.

Stories:
Taste
Lamb to the Slaughter
Man from the South
The Soldier
My Lady Love, My Dove
Dip in the Pool
Galloping Foxley
Skin
Poison
The Wish
Neck
The Sound Machine
Nunc Dimittis
The Great Automatic Grammatizator
Claud's Dog
  - The Ratcatcher
  - Rummins
  - Mr Hoddy
  - Mr Feasey

Standout Story:

While "Lamb to the Slaughter" is perhaps the most famous story from this collection (and for good reason), "The Great Automatic Grammatizator" might be the most relevant to today's reading audience. In this story, two unscrupulous publishers invent a machine that automatically produces stories using a grammar-based mathematical equation, thereby negating the need for living writers altogether. Although written years ago, the themes in this story can be applied to modern-day anxieties about the current publishing landscape and speak to the alleged decline of originality and creativity in the interest of making a fast buck.

Next, read...

2. *Kiss Kiss* (1960)

The tales in this collection, which focus on dishonest relationships between friends, lovers, family members, and even perfect strangers, are more macabre than the previous collection - the twists are more shocking, and the comeuppances are more brutally satisfying. Dahl's expertise at using irony is showcased here, as well as the narrative tension that he builds up so deliciously.

Stories:

The Landlady
William and Mary
The Way Up To Heaven
Parson's Pleasure
Mrs. Bixby and the Colonel's Coat
Royal Jelly
Georgy Porgy
Genesis and Catastrophe
Edward the Conqueror
Pig
The Champion of the World

Standout Story:

While I loved all of these stories, "The Way Up To Heaven" - about an anxious woman whose emotionally abusive husband continually makes her late for important events just to spite her - has an immensely gratifying payoff with a touch of dark humor and a whole lot of poetic justice.

Now, if you think you're ready, move on to...

3. *Switch Bitch* (1974)

Dahl's true potential for the subversive shines through in these four stories, which are considerably longer than most of the stories in other collections, as well as increasingly lecherous. The general themes of these stories revolve around sex, deception, sex, degradation, sex, marital infidelity, sex, sabotage, and did I mention sex?

"The Visitor"
In this story we are first introduced to Uncle Oswald - hedonist, scam artist, and perpetuator of thousands of sexual conquests. (Whose uncle he IS precisely is not revealed.) After Oswald's car breaks down in the desert, a rich stranger invites him to stay in his mansion for the night. Oswald accepts, and is immediately attracted to both the rich man's wife and his daughter, with predictably disastrous results.

"The Great Switcheroo"
Two men who live in neighboring houses switch beds in the middle of the night - without telling their spouses. The goal was sexual adventure, but one of the men is ultimately not happy with the outcome of this horribly deceptive "experiment."

"The Last Act"
A sensitive widow attempts to regain a sense of her former sexuality and confidence with a lover who she knew years ago. She learns, in a humiliating manner, that it will not be as easy as she'd hoped.

"Bitch"
Using (consenting) women as test subjects, the infamous Uncle Oswald and his colleague develop a serum which renders men unable to control their basest of biological impulses. Oswald intends to use the serum on the President of the United States in order to throw him into a scandal. Naturally, his plans go awry.

Although well-crafted and highly entertaining, this collection is not without its problems: mainly, a cringe-worthy and outdated sense of sexism that pervades the narrative. This might merely be a sign of the times in which Dahl was writing, or perhaps it's a reflection of Dahl's deep-seated opinions about women. Whatever the case, these stories will certainly make readers consider the ways in which we handle "controversial" issues in modern day literature, as well as underscore the importance of having conversations about these issues rather than sweeping them under the rug.

Finally, pour a drink, hold on to your hat, and open…

4. *My Uncle Oswald* (1979)

In this first person diary-like account, Oswald, as randy and duplicitous as ever, strives to amass a large fortune by rather questionable means - collecting semen samples from great and powerful men in order to sell the samples to women for the purposes of self-insemination (without the men ever knowing it). To do this, he recruits a science professor with questionable morals, A. R. Woresley, and a former flame, Yasmin, whose morals are, perhaps, even more questionable. Yasmin is used as bait in this scheme, which involves her slipping the targets a potion, causing them to essentially sexually assault her. She then collects the specimens and makes her escape - as the men wonder what the hell just happened. As over the top as this plot seems, the story actually drags in places and, of course, there's the problem of sexism that was discussed earlier in relation to "Switch Bitch." However, it's a relatively quick read, and worth checking out if you want to see Dahl at his most perverse. (Plus, slight spoiler: bad behavior is not rewarded at the end of this book, which makes for a satisfying conclusion to the Uncle Oswald franchise.)

If you're interested in reading an even-handed and detailed non-fiction look into Dahl's life and career, I recommend *Storyteller: The Authorized Biography of Roald Dahl* by Donald Sturrock (2010). But no matter what you may think about Dahl the man or the controversial aspects of his work, his fiction has undoubtedly had a huge impact on the literary world and an immeasurable influence on peoples' reading habits across the decades. In conclusion: reader beware, and enjoy.

JENNIFER EGAN

by Kit Steinkellner

There are so many ways to go wrong. All we've got are metaphors, and they're never exactly right. You can never just Say. The. Thing.

Jennifer Egan
A Visit from the Goon Squad

Jennifer Egan (b. 1962) is an American writer who in just four novels has established herself as one of the most inventive and unpredictable authors working today. Her experiments with form and structure in A Visit from the Goon Squad *won over critics and readers alike, and the linked-short story/novel won both the Pulitzer Prize and The National Book Award.*

As a book reviewer, one of my favorite parts of the job is finding that one adjective that perfectly sums up what makes an author extraordinary. I read my first Jennifer Egan novel when I was in eighth grade (*Invisible Circus*, her 1999 debut novel), but it wasn't until I was deep into my third Egan novel, *Look at Me*, that I realized what Egan's adjective was.

Prescient. The word appeared in my mind like a light bulb popping up above a cartoon character's head. Jennifer Egan is prescient.

What I was responding to was a key plot point in this 2001 novel wherein Egan basically predicts Facebook, as well as Twitter, Tumblr, the social media revolution in general, years before it occurred.

There are so many other adjectives I'm happy to lob Egan's way. Sharp. Complex. Stylish. Unnerving. Mesmerizing. Human. Still, prescient is the word I keep coming back to as I revisit Egan's work. Time and time again she proves herself to be a Cassandra and a Nostradamus. The page becomes her crystal ball. She's a hybrid creature, part-writer, part-fortune teller. We don't have nearly enough of those.

1. *Look at Me* (2001)

Though Jennifer Egan's debut novel is *Invisible Circus*, I propose that it's her follow-up *Look At Me* where Egan starts coming into her full, well, Egan-ness. Our protagonist is Charlotte, a supermodel whose face is destroyed in a devastating car accident. After undergoing complete facial reconstruction, Charlotte returns to her life in New York City unrecognizable to all who once knew her.

In this novel Egan plays with disparate characters who find their lives intersecting (*Goon Squad* seeds!). The storylines twist and turn to weave a tapestry of 21st century American self-obsession, identity crises, and terrorism (Oh, yeah, in addition to predicting Facebook, this novel came out a week after 9-11, I wasn't blowing smoke about the whole prescience thing).

2. *Emerald City* (1996)

This collection of short stories is so skinny that if it were a person you'd have to tell it to eat a sandwich. The stories range in location from China to Mexico to Africa to downtown Manhattan and all explore people losing and finding themselves in the great wide world. A decade before *Eat, Pray, Love* was a thing, Egan was exploring being an American-abroad-but-not-in-Western-Europe with her scalpel-sharp mind.

3. *The Keep* (2006)

This is my favorite Jennifer Egan novel. So if you're going to pick one off the list, pick this. Like *Look At Me*, *The Keep* juggles storylines with Cirque Du Soleil precision and flair. In one storyline, two cousins, traumatized by a childhood prank gone horribly wrong, meet again as adults. One of the cousins is renovating a European castle with plans to make it a place where one can be completely cut off from modern technology and the outside world. This ends up being exactly as creepy as it sounds. Meanwhile, we're also following a relationship between a teacher and her male student in a prison creative writing class she's teaching. The stories eventually merge in the most creepy and rad way possible. This novel is Hitchcockian in its mastery of tension and prescient (there Egan goes again!) in its prediction of increasing human dependence on modern technology. This novel came out A YEAR before the iPhone, how did it know?

Again, I know that *Goon Squad* won the Pulitzer and is widely considered to be Egan's piece de resistance, and we're getting to *Goon Squad,* we are! I just have to give as much love as possible to *The Keep* while I have your eyeballs, this book is so original and intelligent and gobble-it-all-up-in-one-night-good. If you stopped reading in the middle of that last sentence to go pick up a copy at your local library/indie bookstore… my work is done.

4. *A Visit from the Goon Squad* (2010)

Of course you have to read *A Visit From the Goon Squad*, of course you do. Not just because it won the Pulitzer and greatly expanded the definition of what a Pulitzer-winning novel can be, not just because it (along with *Olive Kitteridge*) ensured the viability of novels-that-are-also-linked-stories, but because it is fun. *Goon Squad* is just so fun.

The stories follow a cast of music world characters from the last century on into the near-future. Every story has a different feel and spin. Some stories are more successful than others (I disliked the dictator and the hat maker story so much it almost ruined the book for me, the world of this chapter just rang so false for me, I'm very picky when it comes to credibility and literary dictatorships) but it's difficult not to stand up and cheer for the gall and sheer balls that made this novel possible.

Fun fact: I listened to this book on audio so I had no idea how cool the PowerPoint presentation chapter was until I flipped through a paperback and saw that chapter in print. Don't listen to this book on audiobook, let me be the guinea pig that endured that experiment for you.

As for what's prescient about this novel, well, I'm still waiting! The book only came out a few years ago! It usually takes the better part of a decade to see exactly what Egan has Cassandra-ed and Nostradamus-ed. Maybe it'll end up being the dictator hat story that comes to pass. In which case I will have to eat my own hat!

Enjoy your Egan! I most certainly have.

DAVE EGGERS

by Greg Zimmerman

Whatever I do, however I find a way to live, I will tell these stories. I have spoken to every person I have encountered these last difficult days...I speak to these people, and I speak to you because I cannot help it. It gives me strength, almost unbelievable strength, to know that you are there.

> Dave Eggers
> *What is the What*

Dave Eggers *(b. 1970) is an American writer who burst onto the literary scene with his memoir,* A Heartbreaking Work of Staggering Genius. *In the years since, Eggers has written short stories and novels, including "non-fiction" novels that tell the stories of real people in novel form. Eggers is also the founder of* McSweeney's *and of 826 Valencia, a national literacy non-profit.*

There aren't too many writers for whom you can remember the exact moment you became acquainted. For me, Dave Eggers is one. It was spring of 2000, I was a few weeks from graduating college, and I was sitting in one of the last classes of a creative writing workshop. The discussion veered from our sorry short stories into some of our favorite book titles. The hipster next to me suggested the title of a new memoir by a writer we'd probably never heard of — Dave Eggers' *A Heartbreaking Work of Staggering Genius.* Reaction in the class was mixed — some, not getting the irony, were like "what a narcissist"; others were like "that's awesome." I was torn, but I was intrigued. It took me another three years to talk myself into reading Eggers' career-launching memoir, but once I did, finishing it over the course of two snowy days in the winter of 2003, I've been a huge fan ever since. He's just cool, man.

Ah, to be Dave Eggers – literary renaissance man extraordinaire and unofficial busiest man in publishing! Even before Eggers burst on the scene with his memoir in 2000, he'd started his own publishing company (the now famous-for-being-super-cool *McSweeney's*), which publishes magazines, a humor website, and of course, books, including Eggers' own mostly well-received novels. He's also written screenplays for movies such as *Promised Land* and *Where The Wild Things Are*.

And he's co-founded with his wife, the novelist and editor, Vendela Vida (if Jonathan Safran Foer and Nicole Krauss are the literary royal couple of New York, then Eggers and Vida are the literary power couple of the Left Coast), a charitable writing center and literacy foundation called 826 Valencia.

Is there anything the man can't do? What follows is a reading pathway to get you acquainted with the Eggers oeuvre. If you're interested in some of his essays or shorter work, all you have to do is make a mad dash for Google. His stuff is not difficult to find.

---

1. *Zeitoun* (2009) and *A Hologram For The King* (2012)

Eggers' 2009 nonfiction book *Zeitoun* is a good introduction to Eggers for two reasons. First, it shows you a pared-down, bare bones, no-frills style that appears on and off in Eggers' work. Secondly, it's just an amazingly absorbing (and ultimately rage-inducing) story, and it shows you how Eggers uses literature to teach about injustice, and effect change. The book is about a Syrian immigrant and New Orleans resident named

Abdulrahman Zeitoun, who is wrongfully arrested and jailed by racist law enforcement officers in the aftermath of Hurricane Katrina. Eggers donated all proceeds from the book to a charity he co-founded with the title character called The Zeitoun Foundation. (The foundation has since been shuttered. Zeitoun was arrested in 2012 for allegedly attacking his ex-wife with a tire iron, and then later, hiring a hit man to kill her. In July 2013, he was found not guilty.)

A Hologram for the King is told, as well, in unadorned, simple prose. The 2012 National Book Award finalist is the story of a business consultant who goes to Saudi Arabia to try to sell a telecommunications system to King Abdullah. The novel's a comment on the effects of globalization. It's an allegory of America's (declining?) place in the world. And it's kind of an Office Space on downers. Opinions were slightly mixed on this novel, but like Zeitoun and What Is The What (more on that below), it's typical Eggers — the story is a message and the message is a story.

2. A Heartbreaking Work of Staggering Genius (2000)

While Eggers' 2000 memoir is his most famous work, it's also his most polarizing. It's the story of his move to San Francisco (from suburban Chicago) after both his parents' deaths from cancer within a month of each other. He does his best to care for his younger brother Toph (Eggers is 24, Toph is 11) and laments the fact that he can't spend his time drinking, womanizing, and generally colliding with mid-20s life. He starts a magazine called *Might*, agonizes over whether it will be successful (should he fake a celebrity's death to gain publicity for the magazine?), and even tries out for the third season of MTV's *The Real World*.

As is the case with many memoirs, Eggers took some liberties with actuality and chain-of-events — and that seems to drive people bonkers. Not me, though. Additionally, the book is often glib and dickish, and it includes moments of what could be interpreted as pure vanity and narcissism (exemplified by the title!), which some readers take at face value and insist are a huge turn off and clear examples of Eggers' pretentiousness.

I'd disagree, rather wholeheartedly. To me, these moments – when Eggers discusses his own amazing intelligence and wit, when he positions himself as firmly anti-establishment — are meant ironically. And if read ironically, they're hilarious, because they're so self-deprecating. What's more, these moments are offset by instances of real self-awareness and intense self-doubt — as when and he and other characters talk directly to his readers, often about the process of writing the book itself, and often about whether or not he is a good guardian to Toph.

In sum, this memoir is illustrative of a wonderful writer with a few quirks but just beginning to access an immense talent. It's a super-fun, often poignant, read and a good juxtaposition to the third suggestion here.

3. *What Is The What* (2006)

Eggers' best and most engrossing novel — a 2006 National Book Critics Circle Award winner — tells the story of the refugees of the Sudanese Civil War, but particularly the story of Valentino Achak Deng. Eggers seams together Deng's childhood escape from Sudan with his modern life in Atlanta, among other Sudanese known as the Lost Boys. Eggers is at his brilliant best here — we are seared by Deng's story. He's a good person, but bad things keep happening to him, and so naturally, he is constantly questioning God. This novel is not just essential Eggers, it's essential reading, period.

Like *Zeitoun*, all proceeds from the sales of this novel are donated to a charitable foundation Eggers and Deng founded — it's called The Valentino Achak Deng Foundation, which works to increase access to education in South Sudan.

Other works of note: Eggers' first novel, 2002's *You Shall Know Our Velocity*, about two friends who try to give away a bunch of money, is probably his least-read work. *The Wild Things* (2009) is a short novel based on Maurice Sendak's *Where The Wild Things Are*, and is a companion to the screenplay he co-wrote with Spike Jonze. Finally, Eggers latest novel, *The Circle* published in October 2013 about a woman working at a Google-like company, is a suspenseful contemporary tale about "memory, history, privacy, democracy, and the limits of human knowledge."

WILLIAM FAULKNER

by Jeff O'Neal

Because no battle is ever won he said. They are not even fought. The field only reveals to man his own folly and despair, and victory is an illusion of philosophers and fools.

William Faulkner
The Sound and the Fury

William Faulkner (1897 – 1962) is best known for his novels and short stories, though he also wrote poetry, screenplays, and drama. He won two National Book Awards, two Pulitzer Prizes, and the 1949 Nobel Prize in Literature. When the Modern Library assembled its list of the 100 greatest English-language novels of the 20th century, three of Faulkner's made the list.

Is Faulkner the most intimidating American writer? Maybe even in all of English prose? Shakespeare is certainly difficult, but much of that is the language drift between the 16th century and today. Melville? Sure *Moby-Dick* is enormous, but it isn't disorienting in the same way that Faulkner is. Perhaps only Joyce presents a challenge equal to Faulkner's most demanding novels, though there is a strain of comedy in Joyce that can offer relief.

So what makes Faulkner so tough? Well, it's several things. First, no author I've ever read is as willing to mystify the reader so completely. Seriously, there is a good chance that you will go 50 pages into *The Sound and the Fury* and have no idea what is going on or where it is going on. And once you get your bearings somewhat, you are mostly experiencing the world just as the characters are, and much as we don't go around actually thinking and saying what it is that is bothering and motivating us, neither do Faulkner's characters. The effect then is to be dropped into the flowing-river of another person. And oh what people they are.

Perhaps that's the first and most useful thing I can offer here: do not think that because you are lost that you aren't getting it. Being confused and a little scared is part of the experience—both for you and for the characters themselves.

1. "The Bear" (1942)

This long short story gives you some purchase into Faulkner's thematic concerns, even as the plot and narration are much more conventional than the novels we'll get to in a minute.

Issac, the main character in the story, is a young boy growing up in the South who loves hunting, woodlore, and the kinds of exploration the wild has to offer. "The Bear" of the title is Old Ben, a monster of a bear that is rumored to be immortal and a legend among the hunters and trappers that Isaac looks up to. Determined to hunt Ben down, Isaac is unable to find a dog that will track the bear, but when he finally does, there is an epic confrontation.

Faulkner had a complicated relationship with the South; it was his home, but its practices and history were in many ways distasteful to him, and what becomes of Old Ben, and Isaac's reaction to it, encapsulate this fraught duality.

2. *As I Lay Dying* (1930)

After Addie Bundren dies, her husband and her sons set off to honor her wish to be buried in her hometown. Sounds simple enough, right? Well, try 15 narrators over the course of more than 50 chapters. The near frantic shifting of perspective is mitigated somewhat by the landmarks of the journey; the slow march of the Bundrens to Addie's burial grounds provides ballast for the otherwise fragmented narration.

The title comes from a line in *The Odyssey*, and that allusion offers an interpretive foothold. Where is home? What do I want? What dangers should I be looking out for? Who are allies and who are enemies and will I be able to tell them apart? How much control over my destiny do I have? This perhaps is Faulkner's greatest gift; he has the ability to imbue the banal tribulations of flawed people with biblical weight.

As I Lay Dying is one of the more memorable reading experiences you are likely to have, with a half dozen moments that will stick with you forever.

3. *The Sound and The Fury* (1929)

Here it is: the great American monument of literary modernism that stands shoulder to shoulder with *Ulysses* and *Mrs. Dalloway*.

But while *Mrs. Dalloway* and *Ulysses* take place over very compressed times, *The Sound and the Fury* spans decades as it traces the decline of the formerly aristocratic Compson family in Jefferson, Mississippi. One thing to know is that the first of the novel's four sections is the most difficult. Narrated by Benjy Compson, who has some sort of mental disability, it is a nonlinear, associative tour of more than 20 years of Compson family history as remembered by someone who is unable to process what has gone on around him. Each of the following sections of the novel become easier and easier to follow, if not equally easy to interpret.

It can be helpful too to think of the Compson family itself as "The South," and each of the family members (and neighbors and servants) as personifications of various qualities and conditions of the South in the early 20th century. Faulkner and the Compsons themselves are so attuned to the imposition of the past on all present action and future possibility that the compression and fragmentation of time in the narrative of the novel reflects the stunted, damaged, and stubborn condition of the South as an idea.

If you find *The Sound and the Fury* rewarding, *Absalom, Absalom!* extends the Compson family story, but in terms of reading Faulkner, you've scaled the summit, so the remaining foothills should pose no danger to you. Choose them at your leisure.

JOHN GREEN

by Cassandra Neace

Books are the ultimate Dumpees: put them down and they'll wait for you forever; pay attention to them and they always love you back.

John Green
An Abundance of Katherines

John Green (b. 1977) is a New York Times' Best-Selling author, a Printz award winner, and one-half of the hugely popular Vlogbrothers YouTube channel.

———————————————

The danger when writing realistic novels is that readers will assume that an author is writing about him or her self. Readers understand that they may not be getting the whole picture, but they cannot help but wonder how much of the author can be found in the protagonist. In most cases, they'll never really know.

In the case of John Green, however, it is safe to say that there are hundreds of thousands of people who have a pretty good idea just how much of himself he leaves in his books. They are the loyal Nerdfighters who have been watching his Vlogbrothers channel since it debuted in 2007.

Through the back and forth video conversations that John has with his brother Hank, viewers have really gotten to know him. They can easily imagine what he was like during those awkward teen years. He may not have had the exact experiences described in his novels, but it's clear that he remembers what it was like to deal with all that angst.

For some adult readers, the rumored presence of this "angst" in his novels was enough to put them off for a while, but his most recent novel, *The Fault in Our Stars*, seemed to break through that barrier. The skeptics were won over, and his novel became one of the top sellers of

2012. *Time Magazine* put it at top of their list of that year's best fiction.

It was the pre-publication buzz surrounding the novel and the cross-country tour that he and his brother went on to promote the book that caught my attention. After sitting in the audience for one of the most enjoyable author events that I have ever attended, and then waiting in line for nearly two hours for an autograph, I decided to see what all the fuss was about. Turns out that it was about a really awesome story. And it's where you should start when you want to read books by John Green.

1. The Fault in Our Stars (2012)

The Fault in Our Stars tells the story of Hazel and Augustus, two teens with cancer. But it's not a cancer book. It's a love story. She assumes that she is living on borrowed time, and he has a thirst for life that is contagious. They meet at a support group for kids with cancer, and though they seem as different as two people could be, they are drawn together. Augustus pursues Hazel enthusiastically, but she resists – at first.

The story does have its moments where it seems to be too much. But, these are two kids who have had to live through more than they should have and who may not have their whole lives ahead of them. It makes sense that there are grand gestures and profoundly wise statements. They have to live their lives in fast-forward.

They're going to seem more grown up than the average teenagers. The big C always changes things.

The Fault in Our Stars is Green's finest work. He wouldn't let it out into the world until it was perfect, because it was inspired by a real girl who was really sick and who a made a tremendous impact on his life. Just watch him talk about Esther in his videos. He gets emotional, and that emotion is there on every page of *TFiOS*.

If you don't care for *TFiOS*, then I would probably stop here. His other books are really good, but they probably won't be in your wheelhouse. If you at least appreciate *TFiOS*, then read on. I recommend *Looking for Alaska* for your next read.

2. *Looking for Alaska* (2005)

Looking for Alaska was Green's first novel, and is based on some of his experiences at boarding school. It's pretty personal in that way, and there are hints of the emotional complexity that is found in *TFiOS*. There's a reason that he won the Printz Award his first time out, and why the novel found its way to the New York Times bestseller list seven years after it was originally published.

3. *Paper Towns* (2008)

After that, pick up *Paper Towns*. It's a little high on the angst scale, but it's a nice story with a fairly happy ending. When I was reading Rainbow Rowell's *Eleanor and Park*, I couldn't help but think of *Paper Towns*. They aren't all that similar, but there is something about both books that left me feeling...hopeful. They show that things can and will get better. If you liked one, then you'll probably like the other.

If I haven't convinced you to give Green's books a try, then go and watch the most recent Vlogbrothers video on YouTube. Or one of his Mental Floss lists. Or Crash Course. Or...well, let's just say that John Green is everywhere. And there's a good reason for that.

URSULA K. LE GUIN

by Jenn Northington

Truth is a matter of the imagination.

Ursula K. Le Guin
The Left Hand of Darkness

***Ursula K. Le Guin* (b. 1929)** *is a hugely beloved and prolific author of science fiction and fantasy novels and short stories, as well as an accomplished poet and essayist. She's received numerous awards and honors including the Hugo, Nebula, National Book Award, and Newbery Honor.*

Vacation in the many wonderful universes of Ursula Le Guin! Perfect for the traveler seeking both adventure and culture, feats of derring-do and philosophical conundrums, these lands are full of the unexpected. Marvel at the diverse planets of the Hainish Ekumen; sail the Archipelago of Earthsea; peek into the possible future; all this and more awaits you!

Start out in ***The Wizard of Earthsea* (1968)**, where the young wizard Ged will be your guide. He's only just learning to use his magic, so watch out! There might be some mishaps but don't worry, everything will probably be just fine. You'll begin your journey in his quaint home village and learn some of the traditions of the islands. Then, visit the Masters on Roke, and get a crash course in the Old Speech. Gentlemen only; sorry ladies, it'll be a few books before you too can participate. After Roke, go dragon-hunting in Pendor and riddle with Yevaud. Learn the art of shapeshifting on Osskil, then take to the open seas and explore the borders of life and death. It will be a journey you'll never forget! (Travel insurance recommended.)

Next on your itinerary is **The Lathe of Heaven (1971),** in beautiful Portland, Oregon. Overshadowed by the majestic Mount Hood, Portland is home to three million inhabitants; it's pretty cozy, so you'll be sure to make new friends. Don't forget your umbrella, as in this timeline it never stops raining. While you may be tempted by the recreational substances available to you, we recommend abstaining as side effects can occur. But do come prepared to talk about your dreams! Your guides, George Orr and William Haber, are exactly the folks you'll want to discuss them with. If you're lucky Haber will introduce you to the Augmentor, a piece of fascinating technology that can enhance brain waves. Experience several new realities as Orr dreams them up! Hold onto your hats, because some of them are pretty wild. A copy of the *Tao Te Ching* may be useful in deciphering the various changes you observe. Please note: the reality you arrive at may not be the same as the reality you started out in.

Bundle up, and get ready for the snowy wastes and fascinating genderless culture of the planet Gethen in **The Left Hand of Darkness (1969**)! Terran envoy Genly Ai will be your tour guide to the country of Karhide. Karhide has a rich history and a long tradition of kings, with "Mad King" Argaven XV currently in power. But do watch your pronouns -- Gethenites are androgynous for the most part and male or female only during *kemmer*, their breeding period. You'll also learn about the Ekumen, an organization of over 80 worlds, as Ai seeks to bring Karhide into the fold. The current strained relationship between Karhide and neighboring Orgoreyn is also an excellent opportunity to learn about the political process, with local politician Estraven as your guide. Then, accompany Genly on a tour of the Orgoreyn prison system. From there, you can trek across the Gobrin Ice with Genly and Estraven and put your winter gear to the test. Keep an eye out for snowstorms and mysterious family secrets, which are common this time of year.

Our last stop on the itinerary, **The Wind's Twelve Quarters** (1975), offers a smorgasbord of options for the discerning traveler. You can return to Gethen with "Winter's King" and meet another Argaven. Or, you can visit other stopping points in the Hainish Universe with "Vaster Than Empires and More Slow" (pack a machete and a copy of Marvell's poetry), "The Day Before the Revolution" (brush up on your Proudhon and anarchy), and "Semley's Necklace" (watch mythology in action!). Longing to return to Earthsea? Discover more of the islands with "The Word of Unbinding" and "The Rule of Names." Please note, however, that we strongly advise steering as clear as possible of the local wizardry. Head back to our Solar System with "April in Paris" (all stops in local time), "The Field of Vision" (be on the lookout for conversion experiences), and "Nine Lives" (learn more about the wonderful possibilities of cloning). For the full tree experience, there isn't a better destination than "The Direction of the Road." You can also explore new environments with "Darkness Box," "Things," "The Stars Below," and others!

Now that you've started your explorations and seen some of the wonders that Le Guin's lands have to offer, we know you won't want to stop there. We offer several other vacation packages, tailored to any interest!

- Explore Like an Envoy: *The Telling* and *Four Ways to Forgiveness*
- The Earthsea Extended Tour: *The Tombs of Atuan*, *The Farthest Shore*, *Tehanu*, and *The Other Wind*
- Tiberian Holiday: *Lavinia*
- Hops, Skips, and Jumps: *The Unreal and the Real*, *The Compass Rose*, *A Fisherman of the Inland Sea*, *The Birthday of the World: and Other Stories*

COLUM MCCANN

by Preeti Chhibber

Literature can remind us that not all life is already written down: there are still so many stories to be told.

Colum McCann
Let the Great World Spin

Colum McCann (b. 1965) is an Irish novelist and short story writer. He's written six novels and two collections of short stories, winning the National Book Award for 2009's Let the Great World Spin. He writes about people and their stories from his home in New York. When he's not writing award-winning novels, he teaches at the MFA program in Hunter College.

Colum McCann is, quite simply put, a man of beautiful words. His interviews are always filled with his belief in the "democracy of stories" and the importance of tales. He understands the importance not necessarily of writing, but of the tradition of stories for writers and readers alike. As a reader, it makes him relatable. He gets it.

And boy does the man get his writing. When McCann writes, the writing becomes its subject. In *Dancer*, the text moves through paragraphs choreographed and free form, with *Zoli*, the words are poetic and not to be trusted. His words are inhabited by the specters they're describing.

McCann is not a difficult writer to read. He'll draw you in with beautiful language and imagery and before you know it, you're halfway through the book and fully immersed in his world.

He's no stranger to awards; he was honored in his homeland of Ireland with the International IMPAC Dublin Literary Award, and *Let the Great World Spin* won the National Book Award in 2009.

1. *Dancer* (2003)

Dancer came about because McCann heard the story of a poor Dublin boy holding a television on which Rudolf Nureyev happened to be dancing. And it was the image of this young kid holding the world's greatest dancer in his arms that gave him the point from which he could build the story.

Dancer is the story of Nureyev and his infamy, but it's also more than that. It's a story told through perspective (something McCann uses frequently in his writing), so while Nureyev is the focus, all the other points matter. We don't even start with Rudy, we start with an old Russian woman who is tending to soldiers fallen during WWII. During this story, Rudy is a side note, a Cossack child who performs for the soldiers at the hospital for sugar cubes. This old woman happens to live near some exiled comrades, one of whom will become Rudy's dance teacher. When you read Colum McCann, you read entire lives. You won't know that you're doing it, but you are. And when you get Rudy's perspective (rare though it is), it will speak so much more truthfully, because it will feel like you've been entrusted with this character's story.

It's a beautiful book to start with and an interesting read that serves as an introduction to McCann's rhythmical prose. It was my first McCann, picked up on a whim when I was 18. I fell headfirst into the writing and never looked back. It was the focus on style and story that made me love it because the words he chose were as important as the story they told.

2. *Zoli* (2006)

Zoli is the story of a fictional Romani poetess/singer set in the decades between the 1930s and the early 2000s. It's about Eastern Europe, and Gypsies, prejudice and war, culture and gender. It's also about the printed word versus the spoken word and the unreliability and chains of both.

It's a great follow up to *Dancer* because the basis is in art. You're moving from a person who can't live without dancing and performing, to a woman who loves her art but not cementing it into pages and physical representations. Zoli and Rudy are not so different, both revealed through their determination and stubbornness.

The true difference comes in the narrative. We learn Zoli's story first through a third person narration of Zoli's childhood. Of losing every one of her family members, save her grandfather, and of growing up in the nomadic lifestyle of the Romani. Of discovering music. The second part of the novel is from the perspective of Swann, an Englishman turned Slavik who loves Zoli, but not enough to sacrifice her printed poetry (a sin for the Romani) for her life amongst her people. Lastly, we get Zoli's story told from her own pen, written for her daughter, and of rediscovering her songs towards the end of her life in a place she'd dreamed of seeing.

3. *Let the Great World Spin* (2009)

McCann's 2009 National Book Award winner is loosely based around the very real story of the man who walked between the twin towers and the fictional trial of a New York City prostitute. It harkens *Dancer*'s style with it's varied points of view, but instead of leading you loosely through the story of one person, you're seeing how one event affected people all over the world and the other event is affected by those people.

As I mentioned, we get perspective in *Dancer*, but it can almost be considered limited in comparison to *Great World*. Through the eyes of Corrigan, an Irish priest living among prostitutes in the Bronx, Tillie, one of the aforementioned prostitutes, grieving mothers mourning their sons lost to Vietnam, and many others, we're connected to the political and cultural facets of a moment in time. And through the events happening in the novel, these characters are connected to each other.

This book works well after *Zoli*. We move from the story of one woman, whose art defined a point in her life, to the stories of many, whose lives are defined (in this narrative) by the actions of one artist. The pivotal point in time is that day in August 1974 when Philippe Petit strung up that tightrope. While it uses this day as its basis, the novel moves back and forth in time to build a story of grief and loss that runs through the lives of each protagonist.

4. *Transatlantic* (2013)

The last book on this list is McCann's most recent. *Transatlantic* is what it sounds like: the passage from one side of the Atlantic to the other and back again. The story is told in two parts. We meet two young Great War veterans attempting the first transatlantic flight, then Frederick Douglass, touring Ireland to drum up support for his enslaved brethren, and lastly Senator George Mitchell, trying to broker a peace treaty in Northern Ireland in the late 1990's. At first, the only connection these stories seem to have are men coming into Ireland.

And then Part 2 starts. Lilly Duggan, an Irish maid who in Part 1 is so inspired by Douglass that she packs up and heads to America. She is our first American story of the book. I don't want to spoil any part of this novel, but the connections made between two parts of the book and the people in them are astounding. If *Let the Great World Spin* is about people being affected by a moment in time, then *Transatlantic* is about having people act as conduits for the passage of time and space. It's about history and geography and how people shape both these things.

CHINA MIÉVILLE

by Jenn Northington

Art is something you choose to make... it's a bringing together of... of everything around you into something that makes you more human, more khepri, whatever. More of a person.

China Miéville
Perdido Street Station

China Miéville *(b. 1972) is an English novelist, academic, and short story writer. He has said that his goal is to write a book in every genre, from high fantasy to sea-stories. His 2010 novel,* The City & The City *won the Arthur C. Clarke award and the Hugo Award.*

I'll admit it up front -- I didn't know China Miéville's work before it was cool. He was on my radar, people I knew were reading and loving his books, but no one ever sat me down and said, "Listen, Jenn. You, of all people, need to read these books." (More is the pity!) And when I did finally read one of his novels, it was because my boss pulled a copy of *The City & the City* from a priority stack of galleys and said, "Here, read this one, someone should take a look." Not the most hardcore of beginnings for an author who is now in my Top Ten -- but whatever works, am I right?

Miéville's work has a reputation for being awesome, but also for being difficult. His vocabulary is intimidatingly large; he's got no qualms about dropping you into the middle of the story and letting you find your own way; he plays with voice and structure as a matter of course; and his plots tend to revolve around arcane points of theory. But all these things are also what make his books so great to read. The phrase 'mind-blowing' applies; after finishing one of his books, I have frequently felt like pieces of my brain were leaking out my ears. I've read a lot of science fiction and fantasy, and I mostly know that "Where do they get their ideas?" is a silly question to ask because the answer is usually something like "Well I was on my way home from the pub and I saw a frog on the side of the road and…", but seriously, where does this man get his ideas? If you told me he had a magic wardrobe that took him to strange and terrifying lands and he brought everything back from there, I would not doubt you. The reality, that he just comes up with these things, is almost harder to believe.

If you're not already a visitor to the weirder reaches of sci-fi and fantasy that his work inhabit, you're going to need a guide. My attempt at a map is below -- you can begin at any of these points and find your way from there, but I've suggested follow-ups for each, just in case. I assure you that, while you may occasionally get turned around and find yourself in places you did not intend to go, it's well worth the trip. And if you have already visited the area (by way of, say, Nick Harkaway, Catherynne Valente, Samuel Delaney, or granddaddies Borges or Lovecraft) but haven't gotten to this particular locale, I say to you: "Listen. You, of all people, need to read these books."

1. *Perdido Street Station* (2000)

Between the awards it has won and its incredibly comprehensive world-building, it's impossible not to recommend this book. You'll discover Bas-Lag, a gleefully riotous world inhabited by humans and metahumans and definitely-not-humans that runs on both steam and thaumaturgy. Hefty doses of horror and governmental politics build on the urban fantasy elements, and Miéville's prose is dense, playful, and provocative (yes, all at once). The less you know about this book going into it, the better the reading experience, but let me just say that the Weaver is one of those bona fide Miéville constructions: a villain that runs on philosophy and is all the more terrifying for it. Further along the urban fantasy road: The rest of the Bas-Lag series (*The Scar, Iron Council*) and *Kraken*.

2. *The City & the City* (2009)

Since this was my own personal starting point, I can't not pick it. And while almost every genre novel has a mystery or puzzle at its heart, *The City & the City* has an actual murder mystery! Think Chandler-esque noir plus *The Twilight Zone*, and you'll almost be there. A police procedural that is also a meditation on international politics, societal taboos, and patriotism-gone-awry? Come. On. Fair warning: this book will mess with your mind to the point at which you might see double for a couple hours when you're done. Further along the mind-shattering road: *Embassytown*, which lacks a murder but makes up for it with aliens!

3. *Railsea* (2012)

Theoretically an all-ages book, this novel belongs on your shelf next to *The Phantom Tollbooth*, "Jabberwocky," *Moby-Dick*, *The Odyssey*, and Pullman's *His Dark Materials* series. Miéville's prose always works on a few levels and *Railsea* dials the wordplay up to 11, to the point at which an ampersand is used wherever 'and' would be because it advances the central theme of the book. (Not kidding.) Add to this a dystopic plot that follows three teenagers on the ultimate treasure hunt, and you've got what might be my favorite of all Miéville's novels. Further along the all-ages road: *Un Lun Dun*.

DAVID MITCHELL

by Jennifer Paull

The human world is made of stories, not people. The people the stories use to tell themselves are not to be blamed.

David Mitchell
Ghostwritten

David Mitchell *(b. 1969) is an English author, who has written five novels. After graduating with an M.A. in Comparative Literature from the University of Kent, Mitchell spent eight years teaching English in Japan before he began to make enough from his writing to return to England. In 2007,* Time Magazine *named him one of the 100 Most Influential People.*

Among the ways I'm grateful to have been introduced to David Mitchell's novels, one is that I had no preconceptions when a friend slid *Cloud Atlas* across a table. The name wasn't freighted with superlatives or comparisons, just two iambs. So I'm in favor of ignoring the hyperventilating back-cover blurbs and digging right in.

1. *Black Swan Green* (2006)

Thirteen months in the life of a thirteen-year-old boy, a poetry-writing preteen with a stammer. Stay with me. The narrator, Jason Taylor, unspools thirteen stories of his suburban life: a fracturing family, the social landmines of school, dealing with his "Hangman" speech impediment.

There are striking flashes of language surrounding common experiences, like arcade flirting or a first shave. There's the boy who "eeled forward" to swipe a pack of cigarettes, a girl's "gribbly nipple," or a father's "ironed-in frown." The dialogue sounds completely genuine, especially in the parents' sniping and the kids' boasts and threats. The Falklands War starts and Jason sponges up news and excitement; within a few pages, in a believable about-face, he parrots his sister's more cynical take. And there are realizations that sound familiar to us but keep the freshness of thirteen: "Time in the wood's older than time in clocks, and truer."

Sure, there are nostalgic references to Elvis Costello and Asteroids, but this runs far deeper than, say, Big Star's song "Thirteen." If you enjoy the style, you'll be primed for the *Cloud*-burst.

2. *Cloud Atlas* (2004)

A head-rushing, nesting-doll of a novel. Its six stories enclose each other, moving from the past to the near-contemporary to a vividly imagined far future. I don't think there's any shame in reading the halves together. It's dazzling however you experience it. Mitchell jumps from the journal of a prudish 19th-century lawyer on a Pacific voyage to the letters of a lusty 1930s composer to an interview with a cloned drone set hundreds of years from now. Black humor, chilling predictions, more than a few good intentions warped by circumstance—all galvanized by that essential storytelling hunger for what's next.

Each tale sinks small hooks into the others, so inevitably you start looking for connections and clues. Enjoy them when you find them but you don't need to hunt them down. "Is there such a thing as over-reading?" Mitchell said in his "Art of Fiction" interview, claiming that of *Cloud Atlas's* "echoes, eddies, and cross-references even its author possesses only an imperfect knowledge."

3. The Thousand Autumns of Jacob de Zoet (2010)

By now you may be thinking, "so what's left? Mitchell's done everything!" Not by a long shot. His most recent work could be described as a historic novel, set in a Dutch trading post at Nagasaki, Japan, at the turn of the nineteenth century. But as a more erudite friend described it: It's an encounter narrative, and a captivity narrative, and a transformation narrative, and a tale of suspense, and a political narrative, and a romance…

Where *Cloud Atlas* segments its stories, *Thousand Autumns* blends them. Just when you settle into the rhythm of one narrative, the plot gusts you on to the next. There are tantalizing descriptions through the eyes of the title character, a Dutch clerk. De Zoet is keenly curious about the mostly forbidden world of Japan, so he notices everything from the smell of seaweed to the sound of insects, "tick, bore, ring; drill, prick, saw, sting." He may also beat *The English Patient's* Almálsy for Most Evocative Fruit Eater. The sheer beauty of the language carries into scenes of brutality, medical procedures, and childbirth, inducing squirming admiration.

In his previous books, Mitchell carried a thread or two between novels, as well as within novels. Characters and symbols resurface like slim coins turning up in your pockets or between cushions. Sometimes it's comforting; sometimes it's uncanny. This novel has no overt connections to the others, but the themes of power, predation, and otherness continue to amplify. And it has one of the most poignant final sentences I've ever read.

ALAN MOORE

by Peter Damien

Everybody is special. Everybody. Everybody is a hero, a lover, a fool, a villain. Everybody. Everybody has their story to tell.

Alan Moore
V for Vendetta

Alan Moore *(b. 1953) is considered by many to be the greatest graphic novelist of all time. Moore began his writing career in alternative publications and fanzines, before getting into comics. He is one of the most influential storytellers alive, leaving his mark on both iconic characters and fellow artists.*

You could start reading Alan Moore very easily: you'd just go to a bookstore, and read the Big Obvious books by him, *Watchmen* and *V for Vendetta*, and maybe *Swamp Thing* from there. That'd be just fine (they're as excellent and groundbreaking pieces of work as the hype suggests) but what you might not be able to do after that is move beyond, past the couple of works that get pinned to his name. The fact is that Alan Moore works across a staggering array of subjects, ideas, and even mediums, and I'm not sure someone who just reads *Watchmen* would move comfortably on to the rest of his work. Therefore, I want to try to flex your muscles a little bit.

1. *Supreme: Story of the Year* (2003)

Supreme was an ongoing series forty issues long by the time Alan Moore got hold of it. The first thing he did was throw out everything that had happened and start over. Supreme himself was basically Superman, and rather than try to steer away from that, Moore embraced it wholeheartedly and turned *Story of the Year*, which is just a handful of issues, into a brilliant and funny love-letter to all the comics Alan Moore ever enjoyed.

Throughout the issues, you get flash-backs to old adventures...done in old comic styles, everything from the comic art and storytelling styles of the 40s and 50s, to gleeful places where the comic turns into *MAD* comics, or *Tales from the Crypt*. All the while, we're building and maintaining a huge Superman-esque mythos, with identical-robot-versions of Supreme, a super-powered dog, and so forth. Everything cheesy was embraced, not to be laughed at or mocked, but to be loved and affectionately brought to life again.

It was a breath of fresh air compared to the gritty, chaotic, almost unreadable comics of the 1990s that surrounded this series. It's fairly easy reading, but it introduces you to Alan Moore's vast array of storytelling interests, styles, and capabilities, and this one little volume goes a long way toward preparing you for anything else he throws at you.

2. *Watchmen* (1987)

I don't think we can talk about Alan Moore without discussing *Watchmen*, nor should we, for it is a brilliant comic. I just don't think it's the best place to start with him. It is a grim book that looks at the idea of superheroes and imagines what the real world would be like with them in it, and it is now surrounded by a whole contemporary world of grim, dreary superhero comics. By starting with *Supreme* and coming to *Watchmen* second, you get Moore exploring the lighter, more fun comics that he is discussing in *Watchmen*.

Watchmen is set at the height of the Cold War in the 1980s, and the world is in very bad shape, in complex political fashions that just can't be solved by putting on a costume and a cape and punching a bad guy in the face. Superheroes have had their glory days and have been forcibly retired, but now it seems someone is murdering costumed heroes.

It's an amazing comic, not only full of heroes and social commentary, but full of *people*. Alan Moore's character-work here is as excellent as ever. You might come for the superheroes, but you'll stay for the newspaper vendor who sees everything but is powerless to do anything about it, except talk and talk to a freeloading comic-reading kid sitting by him (they're my favorite characters in the whole story).

More than *Supreme*, *Watchmen* prepares you for the dense complexity of Alan Moore's work. This makes it easier to go on and read his other mammoth projects, like *Lost Girls*, or *From Hell*...and it also enables you to go read some more character driven pieces, like his small comic *A Small Killing*, which is nothing but a brilliant character piece.

3. Promethea, Volume One (1999)

And speaking of complexity, next up we visit *Promethea*, which is possibly my favorite Alan Moore series (it's kind of hard to pick) and also arguably his most dense and complicated comic endeavor...but that complexity doesn't kick in right away, which is why we're only looking at *Volume One*, for the moment.

Promethea is about a young woman named Sophie Bangs who becomes the next Promethea, a goddess of pure story and imagination who can be called into being. It is a sort of magical variation on Wonder Woman, I suppose, but that doesn't really do it justice. It's a science fiction comic, a superhero comic, and eventually turns not only into a meditation on magic, the mind, imagination, gods, and the occult (among other topics) but also gets very experimental as Alan Moore and J.H. Williams III begin seeing just how far they can push the comic medium, and in what directions (and boy do they push it far).

The point of showing you volume one of this comic, though, is that even at the beginning, though fun and fast-moving, the storytelling is a bit dense. There's an awful lot of information packed into the page, everywhere from the complex layouts to all the bits of dialogue, billboards, broadcasts, and other things floating around in the panel. There's a lot to digest, even here at the simpler end of the series. By the time you're through volume one, you're not only ready for more *Promethea*, I hope, but also any of the other complex comics that Alan Moore has done, like the above-mentioned *From Hell*. Easing into dense comics is a skill and a process, just like acclimating yourself to reading very dense and complicated novels, and *Promethea* does that for you. Plus, it's a great deal of fun.

4. *Watchmen* (1987)

You didn't read that wrong. I *have* just recommended *Watchmen* to you twice. The reason is simple: I want you, after a break, to go back and *re-read Watchmen*, knowing that even this re-reading is a stepping stone toward your future Alan Moore reading. The fact is that there is so much in *Watchmen*, it is impossible notice it all the first time. It is very useful to know the end of the story when you go back to re-read the beginning.

Details repeat obsessively throughout the comic. Whether it's panel layouts mirroring each other at the beginning and end of issues, or bits of dialogue and panels echoed at the end and at the beginning, the story is a multi-faceted whole, and the more you know about it when you re-read, the more you'll find within. It keeps resonating off itself with each re-read. I revisit the comic about every six months or so these days, I've lost track of how many times I've read it now, and yet each time I go in, I discover some new connection that I had never noticed before.

This isn't unique to *Watchmen*, either, which is why I want to prepare you to do some re-reading. A lot of his work does this and you will be richly rewarded for re-reading *Promethea*, or *From Hell*, or even the goofy fun stories like *Tom Strong* or the fun-but-dense *League of Extraordinary Gentlemen* stories.

That's it. You're off. There's a tremendous amount of Alan Moore material for you to read. Some of it you may not have even heard of. Go find *The Bojeffries Saga*, which is very funny but I couldn't tell you what it's about. Go find *Halo Jones*, or his work on *Captain Britain*. Heck, I haven't even mentioned the comic milestone and disaster that is *Miracleman*, or *Swamp Thing*, which is where it all really started.

Just read fast. He's still writing an awful lot. We might never catch up at this rate.

TONI MORRISON

by Jeff O'Neal

Sweet, crazy conversations full of half sentences, daydreams and misunderstandings more thrilling than understanding could ever be.

Toni Morrison
Beloved

Toni Morrison *was born Chloe Ardelia Wofford in 1938 in Lorain, Ohio. Widely considered to be one of the most important American novelists, Morrison has written ten novels, two plays, three children's books, and has edited several volumes of essays. In 1993, she was awarded the Nobel Prize in Literature, and in 2012 President Obama awarded her the Presidential Medal of Freedom.*

The only living American with a little thing we like to call The Nobel Prize for Literature, Toni Morrison is not only one of the most important novelists of our time, but also one of the most difficult. Like Faulkner, Morrison isn't afraid to drop you into the middle of something you have no way of understanding. Sometimes it is the middle of some action, but more often it is into somebody's experience of the world. Morrison refuses to simplify the complexity of her characters so that we can understand them immediately. In a way, figuring out what is going on with a Morrison character is almost an ethical act, in that you have to be open and attentive to their history, experience, and motivation.

This is most true of Morrison's greatest novel, *Beloved*, but many readers who start with *Beloved* without any previous experience with Morrison find it a frustrating experience.

Here's my suggested beginner's course in Toni Morrison, with reading *Beloved*, and all of its challenges, as the goal:

1. *The Bluest Eye* (1970)

Morrison's first novel isn't a cakewalk, but the cast of characters is smaller and the plot is easier to follow than the later works. It's also a good introduction to some of her thorough-going concerns and her particular brand of metaphor.

Pecola, the main character, is a young, shy, displaced, abused, and self-loathing girl, who dreams of being white and having blue eyes. Almost a century before *The Bluest Eye*, W.E.B. Du Bois described the "double-consciousness" of black people in America, as they had to see the world both through their own eyes and through those of white people. Pecola has to see the world through three and even four sets of eyes. She has to see the world as a female, as a child, as the victim of sexual violence, and as the mocked outcast of her community. Indeed she must so thoroughly think of herself through other people that whatever it is she is or could be is obliterated.

The destruction and imaginative recreation of characters like Pecola is a through-line of Morrison's fiction.

2. *Paradise* (2000)

If Pecola is a kind of solitary scapegoat, the convent women of Ruby, Oklahoma are a collective scapegoat. *Paradise* is arranged as a series of chapters each focused on a different woman in the town. The central tension of the novel is between the men of Ruby—traditional, rigid, and threatened—and the Convent women, a group of who have taken refuge together seventeen miles out of town, all connected by their displacement from their former lives. Like *The Bluest Eye*, *Paradise* portrays the antagonisms and fault-lines within black communities much more explicitly than it does the direct effects of racism, though it's always lurking around the corner. Where Pecola is undeniably a victim, the Convent women have a more complicated role and more ambiguous fate.

The ending of *Paradise* is excellent preparation for *Beloved*; getting comfortable with ambiguity and confusion is a crucial piece of understanding Morrison's project. It's not just you; it's part of the ride.

3. *Beloved* (1989)

By now, you're accustomed to Morrison's use of violence, her guarded narrative style, and her confounding yet transcendent use of metaphor. *Beloved*'s not going to be easy, but at this point you're well prepared. Morrison is often described as a magical realist, but one thing that distinguishes her in this regard is that her deployment of the fantastical is tactical, occurring only rarely, but in crucial situations and to pivotal characters.

If your experience of reading *Beloved* is anything like mine, there are going to be scenes and images that become part of your reading vocabulary, terrible and beautiful moments that will in some cases have as much force as lived experience itself. Perhaps you can tell that I am dodging saying more about *Beloved*, but that's only because to give anything away is to adulterate the singular experience that reading *Beloved* is and I want to safeguard that.

If you've still got a taste for Morrison after *Beloved*, I'd go *Sula* next and then *Song of Solomon*. At this point I think you can say you've got her major works under your belt. *Tar Baby*, *Jazz*, *Love*, *Home* and *A Mercy* are still all interesting in their own right, but not on the level of the other five.

FLANNERY O'CONNOR

by Josh Corman

I have found, in short, from reading my own writing, that my subject in fiction is the action of grace in territory held largely by the devil.

Flannery O' Connor
Mystery and Manners

__Flannery O'Connor__ (b. 1925) was an American novelist and short story writer. O'Connor was one of the early luminaries of the Iowa Writer's Workshop and close friends with a range of literary notables, from Arthur Koestler to Robert Penn Warren. O'Connor died at the age of 39 from complications due to lupus.

In just eighteen years (her first story was published in 1946 and she died of complications from lupus in 1964), Flannery O'Connor created a body of work that made her name synonymous with the South, short stories, the grotesque, and Catholic fiction. In fact, even mentioning O'Connor's name in reference to another piece of writing bestows upon it an almost unrivalled impression of style and subject. Her work is dark, ironic, funny, violent, bizarre, and shocking, often all at once. Oh, and it's brilliant, too.

I have the impression, however, that O'Connor is an author more admired than read. Yes, her name is often spoken in reverent tones, and her stories are cited as high-water marks of the form by professors in MFA programs everywhere, but she can be hard to approach for a reader. After all, how many great American authors are known almost exclusively as short story writers? But though her novels and nonfiction are less well known, they're no less excellent, and Flannery O'Connor's work deserves to be read as widely as any author of the twentieth century. Which, thankfully, is why you're here.

1. *Mystery and Manners: Occasional Prose* (1969)

Yeah, I know I just told you that Flannery O'Connor's short fiction is what got her name up in lights, so to speak, but authors' nonfiction can often provide readers with helpful intellectual context, a kind of lamp by which the path through their fiction might be lit. It's certainly the case with O'Connor. *Mystery and Manners* features more than a dozen essays, articles, and speeches published posthumously and covering everything from raising her beloved peafowl ("King of the Birds") to teaching literature ("Total Effect and the Eighth Grade") to the intersection of her faith and her vocation ("Catholic Novelists"). O'Connor's dry wit and self-deprecation shine through in every entry, and the effect of spending some time with these pieces is something very like getting to know the quietest girl in class and realizing that she's smarter, funnier, and weirder than you thought possible.

2. *The Complete Stories* (1971)

In 1972, eight years after her death, Flannery O'Connor won the National Book Award for this volume, featuring all thirty-two of her short stories. Short story collections, especially ones this large, can be as daunting as *War and Peace* or *Infinite Jest* to many readers. At least you know to start those on page one, but story collections aren't necessarily best read front to back. *The Complete Stories* deserves its own *Start Here* inside of *Start Here*, and so I'll try to afford it one. Begin with, in no order,

"The Life You Save May Be Your Own," "A Good Man is Hard to Find," "Good Country People," "Everything That Rises Must Converge," and "A Late Encounter With the Enemy." The first four are probably her most well-known pieces, the kind of stuff you may have run into in a textbook at some point, but they also represent O'Connor's prose at it's most hilarious and dangerous. Her famous Southern Gothicism is on full display, and the (often literally) twisted individuals with which she loves to populate her work take center stage. "A Late Encounter With the Enemy" is simply a personal darling, albeit one that tackles one of O'Connor's favorite subjects - the South's fixation upon the Civil War, even into the next century - in a biting critique. If you read and enjoy those five, then you should feel comfortable reading the rest in any order you see fit.

Two final bits of advice, though, on that front. One, if you plan on reading O'Connor's novels (and I hope that you do), then avoid the stories "The Train", "The Peeler", "The Heart of the Park", "Enoch and the Gorilla", and "You Can't Be Any Poorer Than Dead", all of which were repurposed for use in *Wise Blood* (1952) and *The Violent Bear it Away* (1960). Two, whatever order in which you choose to read *The Complete Stories*, take them slow. Imagine the book as a bottle of very fine bourbon, and savor it one glass at a time, letting the complex flavors of every one work their magic.

3. The Novels: *Wise Blood* (1952) and *The Violent Bear it Away* (1960)

O'Connor writes, in her introduction to *Wise Blood*:

> That belief in Christ is to some a matter of life and
> death has been a stumbling block for readers who
> would prefer to think it a matter of no great
> consequence. For them, Hazel Motes' integrity
> lies in his trying with such vigor to get rid of the
> ragged figure who moves from tree to tree in the
> back of his mind. For the author, his integrity lies
> in his not being able to.

This provides a clearer and more powerful description of
Flannery O'Connor's only two novels than I could hope
to. Even more than her stories, O'Connor's novels offer a
distillation of the theological concerns that weighed
upon her mind from childhood until her death. Both
books feature protagonists who attempt to flee,
Oedipus-like, from a God whose reality and presence, in
O'Connor's estimation, cannot be fled. Now, these are
no simple religious allegories or Sunday School lessons.
O'Connor loathed didacticism (as several of her essays in
Mystery and Manners make clear) and isn't about to
abandon those feelings to make it easier on herself or
her readers. Both novels are challenging, deeply strange
portraits of fear, rebellion, grace, and transformation. In
other words, both are pure Flannery O'Connor.

4. *The Habit of Being: Letters of Flannery O'Connor* (1979)

If *The Complete Stories* is a bottle of fine bourbon, and the novels are the entrées, then *The Habit of Being* is a rich dessert. If you've made it through the rest of her work (and if you've gotten to this point, you've read every word the author published during her life), and still crave some O'Connor now and again, O'Connor's letters - written mostly to her friend Betty Hester and her various literary acquaintances - reinforce the icy sharpness of her wit and provide an often fascinating window into her writing habits and her resolve in the face of the illness that took her life.

GEORGE ORWELL

by Tasha Brandstatter

Hitler can say that the Jews started the war, and if he survives that will become official history. He can't say that two and two are five, because for the purposes of, say, ballistics they have to make four. But if the sort of world that I am afraid of arrives, a world of two or three great superstates which are unable to conquer one another, two and two could become five if the fuhrer wished it.

George Orwell
Letter to Noel Willmett,
1944

George Orwell *(1903-1950) was the pen name of Eric Blair, an English novelist, poet, and political journalist best-known for his last two novels,* Animal Farm *and* Nineteen Eighty-Four. *Together they've sold more copies than any other two books by a 20th century author.*

Signs you might be living in an Orwellian world:
- The banks are too big to fail.
- The financial system seems based more on imagination than product.
- Opposing opinions are shouted down instead of debated.
- Politicians rewrite or deny history.
- The government spies on its own citizens.
- The government tortures people, including its own citizens.
- War, or the threat of going to war, is constant.
- A single person stands as the #1 Enemy of the State, yet despite being supposedly hunted he's never caught or killed.
- Free speech doesn't extend to... well, anything.
- Since the words people speak tend to come from their brains, thinking is also probably a bad idea.
- People are arrested when they share facts about the government and its activities.
- LOLcats are illegal (kidding! Everyone loves LOLcats, even in our dystopian future).

Orwell. Orwellian. His very name is synonymous with grim predictions of a future populated with Big Brother, total oppression, and the Thought Police. Unlike the slew of dystopian novels being published today, Orwell's work isn't just a curiosity: it's truly chilling, because he was so damn right about everything.

Think Orwell's vision of the future is outdated and limited to post-World War II paranoia? Get another think. Orwell knew political revolutions and oppressive regimes. He reported on and fought in the Spanish Civil War, was a (polemic) political reporter during the -thirties and -forties, and was virulently anti-Stalinist and anti-Nazi. None of this makes him particularly unique, of course. What does is his understanding of history and human nature: both *Animal Farm* and *Nineteen Eighty-Four* are filled with references to history and memory and the power they have over the present.

Is Orwell still relevant? All you need to do is read his books to know the answer to that question.

---

1. *Animal Farm* (1945)

Animal Farm is one of those kismet books every author hopes to write someday: a brilliant idea, perfectly executed at exactly the right time. Orwell called it a fairy tale; critics call it a satire. Neither description really captures how *Animal Farm* combines a great story, sympathetic characters, and eviscerating socio-political commentary in little more than 100 pages. The premise may seem somewhat silly and simplistic at first—the animals of a farm expel their abusive and lazy human owner with the idea of establishing an equal animal society, only to find themselves in the exact same situation they started in—but that's the genius of the thing: it's simple enough to work as a parable for every uprising from the French Revolution to the recent overthrow of Mohamed Morsi in Egypt. I like to imagine Orwell as speaking to the reader through the jaded donkey, Benjamin, the only animal on the farm with any historical memory who is pretty sure that things will go on they always do, "that is, badly." Naturally Benjamin is right, but not because the animals' ideas are flawed; rather, it's because their system is based on the one that came before. To my mind, *Animal Farm* is Orwell's masterpiece, a perfect distillation of his ideas that's accessible to people of all ages and backgrounds.

2. *Nineteen Eighty-Four* (1949)

While *Animal Farm* is Orwell's vision of a communist society, *Nineteen Eighty-Four* depicts England in the throws of totalitarianism. Admittedly, the two share many characteristics, especially in the mind of Orwell. Winston Smith is a lonely everyman who hates Big Brother, the dictator of Oceania. When he tries to break away from Big Brother and falls in love, he incurs the attention of the Thought Police. Doublethink, Big Brother, Thought Police, and memory hole are just a few of the concepts that first appeared in this book and are now part of our lexicon. Of all Orwell's writings, *Nineteen Eighty-Four* is the one he's most closely associated with. Even the term Orwellian originated with this book. So why should you read *Animal Farm* first? Simply put, *Nineteen Eighty-Four* is not as accessible as *Animal Farm*. It's more about ideas—brilliant ideas—than characters or story, so it's a difficult book to get into. As much as I find doublethink and newspeak (the new language of Oceania that allows people to say anything and mean nothing) fascinating, the first third of the book is slow. Still, if you want a truly chilling vision of our dystopian future and a total synthesis of Orwell's thoughts, *Nineteen Eighty-Four* is a must-read.

3. *The Collected Essays, Journalism and Letters of George Orwell*, edited by Sonia Orwell and Ian Angus (1968)

Sure, you could read one of Orwell's pre-*Animal Farm* novels—the majority of which are more along the lines of fictively rearranged memoirs—but if you want to understand the man and how the ideas of *Animal Farm* and *Nineteen Eighty-Four* developed, *Collected Essays, Journalism and Letters* is the way to go. Published in four hefty volumes (start with the last and work your way backward), the books aren't as intimidating as they look because the writings in this collection spark with cutting wit and a sense of humor that one might not expect from reading *Nineteen Eighty-Four*. There are essays on books and reading, book reviews, snarky response letters, and essays on everything from atomic bombs to economics to the legal system. I think it's safe to say if he were alive today, Orwell would be running a killer blog. It's also fascinating to see just how far back Orwell was thinking of the world of a totalitarian dictatorship that eventually became *Nineteen Eighty-Four*: five years before the novel was published, he was already writing, "two and two could become five if the fuhrer wished it." But by far the best reason to read *The Collected Essays* is that reminds you Orwell was part of the establishment: he was born, raised, and fought as a member of the British empire until he turned his back on imperialism and chose to live as a writer in the poorest parts of London and Paris (Siddhartha much?). That doesn't negate the fact that he spent most of his adult life as a fervent socialist and anti-imperialist; rather, it shows the depth and complexity of his political beliefs. If Orwell is our modern oracle, it's because he comprehended human nature regardless of class or politics.

DOROTHY PARKER

by Andrew Shaffer

If you have any young friends who aspire to become writers, the second greatest favor you can do them is to present them with copies of *The Elements of Style*. The first greatest, of course, is to shoot them now, while they're happy.

Dorothy Parker

Dorothy Parker (1893 – 1967) *was one of the twentieth century's foremost poets, writers, and critics. Known for her biting wit, Parker was a founding member of New York's legendary Algonquin Round Table, an O. Henry award winner, and a two-time Academy Award nominee.*

"I hate writing, I love having written," Parker once said. Despite her avowed "hatred" of writing — and an alcohol habit that forced her to use an undertaker's perfume to mask the smell of liquor on her — she churned out reams of poetry, short stories, screenplays, and criticism in her seventy-three years, a fraction of which is collected in Penguin's *The Portable Dorothy Parker*.

Despite her prodigious output, she never considered herself a real writer on level with her Lost Generation peers Ernest Hemingway and F. Scott Fitzgerald. Real writers, she argued, wrote novels. She worked on a novel for nearly fifty years and died without publishing a word of it. If she had completed it, would her legacy be different?

It's a question worth asking, because Parker is known today primarily for her one-liners. "The first thing I do in the morning is brush my teeth and sharpen my tongue," Parker once said. Her bon mots were made for a platform like Twitter, where they continue to be passed around and retweeted. (Never mind that hundreds of quips are misattributed to her on the Internet, such as this ironic quote: "I don't care what is written about me so long as it isn't true.") The idea of Dorothy Parker is certainly alive and well. If you want to dig below the surface, though, here's where to start...

1. *Enough Rope* (1926)

Parker's first poetry collection was published in 1926. The book was dismissed by *The New York Times* as "flapper verse." Other publications were a little more generous: *The New Republic* said that "she writes well: her wit is the wit of her particular time and place.... Within its small scope, it is a criticism of life."

The somewhat muted critical reception did not hurt sales: *Enough Rope* sold 47,000 copies within a year — a remarkable feat, given that most poetry collections sold no more than 5,000 copies at the time.

Like the critics pointed out, Parker's sardonic verse was in tune with the disaffected "lost generation" of the Roaring Twenties. Still, they don't read as dated. Almost a century later, her lines still crackle with dark wit that wouldn't be out of place in, say, a modern rock song. Here are a few from "Résumé":

Guns aren't lawful,
Nooses give,
Gas smells awful.
You might as well live.

(Parker attempted suicide about half a dozen times. Following one attempt, a friend consoled her in the hospital. "If you don't stop this sort of thing, you'll make yourself sick," he said.)

Enough Rope is collected in *The Portable Dorothy Parker* and Parker's *Complete Poems*.

2. "Big Blonde" (1929)

"Big Blonde" is Parker's best-known short story, which won an O. Henry award in 1929 for best short story of the year. It's also a scathingly autobiographical glimpse into Parker's own alcoholism: "She commenced drinking alone, little short drinks all through the day. She was never noticeably drunk and seldom nearly sober. It required a large daily allowance to keep her misty-minded. Too little, and she was achingly melancholy."

"Big Blonde" is collected in *The Portable Dorothy Parker* and *Complete Stories*.

3. *The Portable Dorothy Parker*, edited by Marion Meade

The Portable Dorothy Parker, edited by biographer Marion Meade (*Dorothy Parker: What Fresh Hell Is This?*), is your one-stop shop for all things Dorothy Parker: short stories, poems, and letters. This volume also collects the best of her literary criticism, including her reviews of works by Oscar Wilde, Leo Tolstoy, Ernest Hemingway, Jack Kerouac, Truman Capote, and John Updike.

The first half of the book was assembled by Parker herself in 1944, giving unique insight into what she considered her best work. The latest Penguin deluxe edition features a glorious wraparound cover and jacket flaps by cartoonist Seth. An interesting sidenote: When you buy a Parker book, her estate's portion of the proceeds go directly to the NAACP.

Depending upon what interests you more from this collection, you can branch out into one of Penguin's companion volumes, *Complete Stories* or *Complete Poems*.

4. *Dorothy Parker: In Her Own Words*, edited by Barry Day

Parker never penned an autobiography, but once joked that if she did, it would be titled *Mongrel*. Thankfully, she often wrote about her own life, enough so that editor Barry Day stitched together this biography using Parker's own words. He sets many of her tossed-off one-liners in context.

"Read her work in total, and a striking personal portrait emerges of a woman perpetually drawn to but disillusioned by love," Day writes in his introduction. "Self-mocking, self-loathing, and deliberately underachieving, lonely and constantly contemplating death and the means of achieving it, her eye perpetually peeled for the dark cloud that invariably accompanies any silver lining."

CHARLES PORTIS

by Liberty Hardy

Nothing is too long or too short either if you have a true and interesting tale and what I call a "graphic" writing style combined with educational aims.

Charles Portis
True Grit

Charles Portis was born in El Dorado, Arkansas, in 1933. His writing career began in college when he worked as a reporter before enlisting in the Marines. He served during the Korean War, and after his discharge, he went back to school and received a degree in journalism. Portis has served as the London bureau chief of the New York Herald-Tribune and a writer for The New Yorker. He is best known for his novel True Grit (1968), arguably the greatest Western ever written, which was adapted as a film in both 1969 and 2010. On the Male American Authors Reclusivity Scale (which is something I just made up) he slightly edges out Cormac McCarthy and Larry McMurtry, and falls in behind Thomas Pynchon.

If slow and steady wins the race, give Charles Portis all the awards. Portis is a master of satire, a comedic genius with an eye for detail. That's not to say his books aren't serious, just that he manages to find the humor in entirely plausible situations before breaking your heart. Just like...what's that thing? Oh yeah. Real life. In what I find the most accurate statement about Portis, the writer Roy Blount, Jr. said, "Charles Portis could be Cormac McCarthy if he wanted to, but he'd rather be funny."

Since the publication of his first novel, *Norwood*, in 1966, there have been only four more published novels, the last in 1991. Could it be that Portis stopped finding the humor in the world? With his eightieth birthday just a few months away, chances are we've got all the books from Charles Portis that he wants to give us. But then, how many other authors could benefit from "less is more" when it comes to releasing novels? (Spoiler: Truckloads.) Here are are the three books that best show the breadth of Portis's oeuvre.

1. *True Grit* (1968)

While I'm tempted to suggest saving the best for last, *True Grit* is so simple in its brilliance, the least convoluted of his novels, that it is perfect for Portis beginners. And for readers who are skeptical of Westerns. Forget that label 'Western': This is the story of a daughter who wants to avenge the murder of her father. It's a Greek tragedy, with spurs. Looking for revenge after her father is murdered by his farmhand, Tom Cheney, headstrong fourteen-year-old Mattie Ross employs Rooster Cogburn, a hard-drinking, one-eyed U.S. Marshal with a reputation for being the toughest gunslinger around. Mattie isn't willing to just send Rooster off with her money in search of Cheney: she insists on accompanying him on the journey to keep him on task (and from stealing her money.) Also along for the trip is a Texas Ranger named LaBoeuf, who has been tracking Cheney for many months. Despite the seriousness of murder and revenge, this is practically a buddy cop story. What struck me about *True Grit* the first time I read it is how funny it is. In my opinion, neither of the films has fully captured just how brilliant this book is. The dialogue is so sharp that it'll cut your brain. I mean that in a good way. And speaking of awesome dialogue, that brings me to the next book.

2. *Norwood* (1966)

Portis's first novel kicks off what is to be a central theme in all his books: the road trip. In each of his books, the central character embarks on a quest, even if it's a small one, in which they encounter colorful characters and danger. In *Norwood*, it's ex-Marine Norwood Pratt. Giving you a description of the book almost feels wrong, because there are so many strange and wonderful aspects, they seem best served as a surprise. But here goes: Norwood is hired by sketchy Grady Fring (The Kredit King) to drive an Oldsmobile from Texas to New York City. Along the way he meets the second-shortest midget in show business, a woman who steals his heart, and a college-educated chicken. (The story of a man falling in love with the second-shortest college-educated chicken is another book entirely. I think John Irving wrote it.) Fans of Elmore Leonard and George V. Higgins will love Norwood the best out of all of Portis's books. Did I say *True Grit* was his best? I take it back. It's *Norwood*. Definitely *Norwood*. And like *True Grit*, it was also made into a film, in 1970, starring Glenn Campbell and...wait for it... football legend Joe Namath.

3. *Masters of Atlantis* (1985)

Okay, really, this is the best Portis book. It is his most absurd and hilarious, and also his smartest. It centers around the Gnomon Society, a fraternal order leading their lives according to text from a book supposedly from the lost city of Atlantis. Lamar Jimmerson is given the book by a shady character while serving in World War I, and finding inspiration is its text, spends his life trying to spread the word. As the order grows, so does the absurdity. Jimmerson's trusty sidekick, Austin Popper, steals the book with his crazy exploits and his talking bluejay, Squanto. Popper pretty much ruins everything he touches without anyone around him realizing what is actually happening. I find *Masters of Atlantis* to be Portis's most Vonnegut-esque, and even a bit Kafkaesque. (Unsolicited recommendation: Readers who love *Masters of Atlantis* should check out *The Teleportation Accident* by Ned Beauman.)

There are only two more published Portis novels: *The Dog of the South* (1979) about a jilted husband who drives to Mexico in search of his wife, and *Gringos* (1991) about an American living the easy lifestyle in Mexico. If I were absolutely forced to choose, *Gringos* would be the one I least recommend, and by least recommend, I mean I would still suggest you read it, because you should sop up every bit of Portis that you can. They're all wonderful.

Bonus Round: For those of you who are now hooked on Portis, or are rabid fans already, there is *Escape Velocity: A Charles Portis Miscellany* edited by Jay Jennings (2013), a collection of essays, short fiction and even a play. (I recommend the paperback edition, as it includes another story not found in the hardcover.) And there's also a great article online by Charles McGrath called

"The Elusive Charles Portis, Author of 'True Grit'", which touches on his cult author status. And Donna Tartt wrote a fantastic afterword in a recent edition of *True Grit* - worth tracking down. Okay, really, I'll shut up now.

PHILIP ROTH

by Jeff O'Neal

We leave a stain, we leave a trail, we leave our imprint. Impurity, cruelty, abuse, error, excrement, semen - there's no other way to be here. Nothing to do with disobedience. Nothing to do with grace or salvation or redemption. It's in everyone. Indwelling. Inherent. Defining. The stain that is there before its mark.

Philip Roth
The Human Stain

Philip Roth (b. 1933) has won two National Book Awards, two National Book Critics Circle Awards, three PEN/Faulkner Awards, a Pulitzer Prize, and the Man Booker Lifetime Achievement Award. In a career spanning more than 50 years, Roth has written 28 novels and two works of non-fiction. In 2013, Roth announced that he was retiring from the writing life.

I'm cheating with this one. To my mind, there are two main thoroughfares through Roth's work: the big social novels and the experimental novels. And rather than do the right, hard thing of charting a course that integrates both of them, I am splitting them up. So I also have the meta-level pathway to suggest: if you are new to Roth, start with the social novels, then move to the more experimental stuff.

Here is my recommended pathway for the social novels:

1. "Goodbye, Columbus" from *Goodbye, Columbus* (1959)

The title novella from his debut collection, "Goodbye, Columbus" holds up. It has many inchoate themes: assimilation, desire, upward mobility, identity, and melancholy. One of Roth's many strengths is his ability to create characters who look across cultural lines. Here, Neil Klugman, a recent college graduate, falls for a young Radcliffe student, Brenda Patimkin, and finds himself in the inner sanctum of 1950s New England gentile-dom. The cultural observer figure seems to get Roth just enough out of his own head to mitigate the solipsism of the Zuckerman books, but without losing his keen eye and lacerating edge. Even as a young writer, Roth is fascinated by the passing of time and what the realization of time's passage does to people. Only now, as Roth's writing career is at the close, can we see how strikingly appropriate that his first major work should have "goodbye" in the title.

2. *The Human Stain* (2003)

The Human Stain is the last novel in a sort-of trilogy with *American Pastoral* and *I Married a Communist*. Here, we get Roth's familiar avatar, Nathan Zuckerman, learning of his neighbor's racially charged dismissal from his teaching position. Coleman Silk has been passing as white for most of his adult life when a casual comment about a couple of black students gets him embroiled in the bureaucratic rage of liberal academia.

Roth excels at seeing the knottiness of American identity, and Silk's story has an almost Greek sense of the tragic and the inevitable. As a long-time target himself of the kind of willful misunderstanding that Coleman Silk experiences, Roth captures the righteous indignation of the quasi-guilty. It's interesting to imagine Roth himself as Silk, aging, sulking, unapologetic, and yet still wounded.

Where "Goodbye, Columbus" is wistful, even elegiac for a way of life receding into the past, *The Human Stain* shows how a lifetime of work can collapse in a moment. It isn't pretty and it isn't sad; it's just ugly—and over.

3. *American Pastoral* (1997)

This is the story of the great Seymour "Swede" Levov, a star Jewish-athlete and childhood idol of Nathan Zuckerman. Zuckerman, returning to Newark for a high school reunion, learns of the Swede's death from Levov's younger brother. The Swede's idllyic life, beauty queen wife and prosperous upper-middle class existence, comes to a sad and crushing end as a result of his daughter's violent act of protest in the late 1960s. Zuckerman becomes fascinated with the story and attempts to fill in the gaps in the story with newspaper clippings, calls to acquaintances, and his own imagination.

American Pastoral finds Roth at the height of his powers: elegiac, biting, funny, dark, flawed, and panoramic. His vision of America as both creator and destroyer of dreams and identity is never more compelling than it is here. To read Roth write about America from the mid-1960s to the mid-1970s is to see one of our master observers survey one of the most important stretches of the twentieth century. The Zuckerman as observer structure in both *The Human Stain* and *American Pastoral* gives Roth the room to stand apart and witness the very trials and times he himself experienced. In earlier novels, Zuckerman seemed more aligned with Roth, but as Roth, and Zuckerman, aged, it became clear that Roth had outgrown him and needed these other projections of Roth's experience, the Swede and Coleman Silk, if he wanted to tell the story of not just who he was, but what he had been a part of.

Zuckerman's imaginary reconstitution of Levov's life gives a glimpse of Roth's more experimental, fabulist work. The questions of identity, art, and experience that suffuse the realistic novels above carry over into his first experimental novel, *The Ghostwriter*, and it is a natural place to transition to that part of his work. From there, it's a short jump to his most accomplished work of near postmodernism in the beguiling, cerebral, and elusive *Operation Shylock*.

SALMAN RUSHDIE

by Jenn Northington

Language is courage: the ability to conceive a thought, to speak it, and by doing so to make it true.

Salman Rushdie
The Satanic Verses

Salman Rushdie (b. 1947) is a British Indian author of
novels, short stories, and essays. His work combines
elements of magical realism with cultural and religious
history. In 1981, he won the Man Booker Prize for
Midnight's Children, *but he became an international
figure after he received death threats for his portrayal of
Islam in his 1988 novel,* The Satanic Verses.

Do you like mythology? How about rock and roll?
Politics and revolution? Puns? Dysfunctional families?
Stories that are about stories? Allow me to introduce you
to my dear friends, the books of Salman Rushdie. There
are many of them, 13 to be precise, which is a lot of new
books to meet. And some of them are quite long, and
rather intimidating, and have big Award Winner stickers
on them, which can make you feel a bit underdressed.
But I assure you, they're well worth getting to know.

1. *Haroun and the Sea of Stories* (1990)

Here, let's start with one of the friendliest ones. Meet
Haroun and the Sea of Stories, which Rushdie wrote for
his son. It's about a boy named Haroun, whose father
has lost his formerly prodigious gift for storytelling. What
starts out as a quest to return his father's Gift of Gab
becomes an adventure complete with a kidnapped
princess, opposing armies of dark and light, a sinister
plot to plug up the Sea of Stories, and many P2C2E
(Processes Too Complicated To Explain). If there is a pun
to be made, it is in here; no legend or fairytale goes

unreferenced; and if you pay attention, there are even bits and pieces for those of us who are Very Grown Up and Literary. A fantastic rainy-day story, *Haroun* is also a primer for the wordplay and scattered references so common in Rushdie's work.

2. *The Ground Beneath Her Feet* (1999)

But where, you ask, is the rock and roll? For that we turn to *The Ground Beneath Her Feet*, which is at base an Orpheus and Eurydice retelling that starts in the fast times of the '60s and barrels right along through the '90s. It's a jetsetter of a book, on tour from Mumbai to London to America and back and forth and beyond. Old World meets New World, East meets West, and everyone is a little nuts. I take it back, a lot nuts. Ormus Cama, our hero, gets his musical ideas from a parallel universe via dreams of his dead twin brother. Vina Apsara, our heroine, has changed her name as many times as her hair color. A master of constant reinvention, she orbits around Cama, who is the love of her life -- but not enough for her, even so.

And our narrator, the photographer Rai, follows in Ormus and Vina's wake, caught up in the momentum but forever off-stage. The stakes are epic, and so are the failures. Cama's family also contains a murderer and a father who can't pull himself out of his obsessive research long enough to parent; Vina, whose mother killed herself and the rest of her family, has bounced through several families and never managed to keep any of them. Rai's own parents, initially the sanest folks in the book, lose themselves and each other as they fight for the architectural soul of Mumbai. Drugs, sex, and music -- above all, music -- pervade the novel alongside succubi, tears in the fabric of reality, friends who look like foes and foes who look like friends. Everyone goes to hell, and not everyone makes it back. This is the book that will take you out to the clubs, rock you all night long, and leave you broken-hearted but never regretting a second.

3. *The Satanic Verses* (1988)

This next one looks pretty dangerous, but trust me: *The Satanic Verses* wants to be your friend. Sure, it's got a reputation. It's a political lightning rod, a thrower of bricks at glass houses, the impetus for a fatwa. It is the book that launched a thousand articles. It has questions -- so many questions -- about religion, philosophy, culture, society, class, race, everything really. If Rushdie is known for any book, it is this book. And this book wants to tell you stories, so many stories. A movie star becomes an archangel, a voiceover actor becomes a demon, a merchant takes to the hills and becomes a prophet, a young woman leads an entire town on a pilgrimage to the sea. There are visions all around, and who can say which are blessed and which are cursed?

This book will grab you by the arm and start telling you one tale, and before you know it that story has branched into two, then four, and then you've lost count and don't know up from down, right from left, back from forward. But you won't care, because the stories are so good, so thought-provoking, and the book so entertaining, all you want to know is: what happens next?

4. *Joseph Anton* (2012)

There's a new kid in the corner over there, you might have noticed. Seems quiet compared to the others, less flamboyant. According to the cover, its name is *Joseph Anton* and it's a memoir. You don't often find one sporting a close third person POV but trust me, you hardly notice. Personally, I recommend hanging with *Joseph Anton* once you've met a few of the others; references, true tales that inspired fictional ones, all become clear, and you've got the joy of finally getting to say, "So that's where that comes from!" Of course, you also get a behind-the-scenes view of Rushdie's life (such as it was) under the threat of the fatwa, as well as a whole lot of great anecdotes about other famous people. But if you must know, now now now!, about all those things then by all means introduce yourself right away.

JAMES SALTER

by Rebecca Joines Schinsky

The polished sentences had arrived, it seemed, like so many other things, at just the right time. How can we imagine what our lives should be without the illumination of the lives of others?

James Salter
Light Years

James Salter (b. 1925) *left the Air Force and began a long and productive writing career in 1956 with the publication of his debut novel* The Hunters. *The nearly six decades since have brought five more novels, two collections of short fiction, a book of poetry, a memoir, collected travel writing, a food book co-written with his wife Kay Eldredge, and multiple screenplays, making Salter one of the most diverse--and perhaps most under-recognized--contemporary American writers.*

Salter is often called "a writer's writer," a reference to his peers' recognition of the caliber of his work, but to subscribe to this notion is to damn him with faint praise. His dazzling sentences tell us, in just a few words, volumes about characters' inner lives, and they demonstrate his remarkable economy of language. Salter's writing is beautiful and his construction elegant. His work is restrained, but it never feels spare; it is controlled, but it seems effortless. That's the greatest and most difficult trick a writer can perform for readers.

Here's the route I suggest for sampling Salter's oeuvre and finding out for yourself why he deserves a place in the modern canon and on every reader's bookshelf.

1. *The Hunters* (1956)

Salter's debut novel about an Air Force pilot in the Korean War is his most straightforward. Captain Cleve

Connell's only goal is to become an "ace," taking down five enemy planes and establishing himself among the elite, but circumstances are never quite on his side. Cleve has a crisis of confidence, and his men have a crisis of faith. The resolution to both is as powerful as it is unexpected. *The Hunters* is a war novel, but you need not know much about war in general or this war in particular to enjoy it. Wars are fought and endured by humans, and Salter is a master at telling human stories. This is a perfect introduction to how he does it.

2. *A Sport and a Pastime* (1967)

Depicting the erotic in literary fiction is a tricky business indeed, and no one does it better than James Salter. Discover his singular sex writing in this novel about a Yale dropout wandering through Europe and the young French woman with whom he enjoys a brief affair. The moments they share are steamy and illicit without ever being vulgar. Salter makes the risqué and even taboo almost irresistibly alluring, and he captures the moment in a relationship when both parties know it will soon end and want to wring every last bit of beauty out of it before it does. Here Salter plays with time and narrative structure as well, providing a glimpse of techniques we'll see again later. Salter has said this is his favorite of his books and the only one that comes close to living up to his standards.

3. Light Years (1975)

The marriage-in-decline story is a literary trope unto itself, and *Light Years* is an exemplary entry into the genre. Main characters Nedra and Viri are in their late twenties when the novel begins. It is 1958, and they are raising two young daughters on an idyllic property outside New York City. Their family life isn't perfect, but it is filled with glittering instants, enough that they are willing to overlook the niggling doubts and nagging dissatisfaction. But marriage is a fragile thing, delicate and easily damaged, and small problems are only small for so long. Salter chronicles several decades in the couple's life, showing us affairs, arguments, attempts at resolution, and, ultimately, divorce. He presents peripheral characters that are just as compelling and fully realized as his protagonists and he moves fluidly between multiple points of view in the same chapter, often on the same page. All of the characters here are flawed and human, and Salter neither blames nor excuses them for their misdeeds. There is nothing unusual or remarkable about how Nedra and Viri grow apart from each other; indeed it is the most common of stories, but Salter's telling of it is gorgeous and nuanced. Read this with a pen in hand, ready to underline breathtaking sentences and admit difficult truths.

Interlude: Salter took a long break from novels, and you might want to do the same before you move on to his ultimate work. Dip into *Dusk* for wonderful short stories that show Salter can be just as effective and memorable in a compressed format. Read his memoir *Burning the Days* for insight into his experiences as an Air Force pilot, the early love affairs that shaped him (the sex writing here is just as good as it is in his fiction), his life as a writer, and his marriage. Take a longer look at the love of travel and European culture that pervades Salter's fiction with *There and Then*, his collected travel writing, or celebrate food with *Life is Meals*.

4. *All That Is* (2013)

Salter's newest novel, published 34 years after his next most recent one (1979's *Solo Faces*), might also be the 87-year-old writer's last. *All That Is* bears all the Salter hallmarks--the incredible sentences, the fully drawn supporting characters, the signature exploration of intimate moments, the generous but hit-you-where-you-live insights about life and relationships--and brings them together in a work that feels like the capstone to a remarkable career. The novel follows World War II veteran turned book editor Philip Bowman through more than six decades as he navigates love, loss, and constantly-evolving American culture. It is also something of a love letter to the publishing industry and the transformative power of books. Salter may be a writer's writer, but he is also a reader among readers.

> He liked to read with the silence and the golden color of the whiskey as his companions. He liked food, people, talk, but reading was an

inexhaustible pleasure. What the joys of music were to others, words on a page were to him.

James Salter. He knows.

JOHN STEINBECK

by Benjamin Anders

And this I believe: that the free, exploring mind of the individual human is the most valuable thing in the world. And this I would fight for: the freedom of the mind to take any direction it wishes, undirected. And this I must fight against: any idea, religion, or government which limits or destroys the individual. This is what I am and what I am about.

John Steinbeck
East of Eden

John Steinbeck (1902-1968) wrote sixteen novels, five short story collections, and six non-fiction books. Much of his most famous work was set in and around his hometown of Salinas, California. In 1962, he was awarded the Nobel Prize in Literature.

With *Of Mice and Men* and *The Grapes of Wrath* being as commonplace as they are in the respective book-bags of high school freshmen and seniors, a guide into the labyrinth of greater Steinbeck-dom might not seem like the most obvious one. The first thing to know about Steinbeck is that he was incredibly prolific, with sixteen novels to his credit, many of them quite long and delicately structured. The other thing I like to say (or to claim more accurately) is that unlike most authors of upwards of ten novels, nearly all of Steinbeck's sixteen are brilliant, though only a few are widely read.

1. *Cannery Row* (1945)

I will only list one that is a common favorite, because it is so dear to me. I discovered Steinbeck not in a classroom but on a family trip through the Salinas Valley, the famed Central California setting that takes on a near mythic quality in most of his work. I was not more than fifteen at the time, and I have a rare lucid memory of my mother reading through *Cannery Row* as the farmlands whirled by my window and my father drove North. I was just beginning my love affair with literature at this age, and I remember being struck by the simple music of

Steinbeck's language as I am struck by it now as I open the book again to its most famous passage:

> Cannery Row is the gathered and scattered, tin and iron and rust and splintered wood, chipped pavement and weedy lots and junk heaps, sardine canneries of corrugated iron, honky tonks, restaurants and whore houses, and little crowded groceries, and laboratories and flophouses.

The discovery of Steinbeck coincided for me with the discovery that language could accomplish than I knew. I suggest that the reader, no matter her age, begin where I began--with *Cannery Row*.

Here, Steinbeck concerns himself most singularly with the theme of giving an account of place, of a town, of a town's gathering and scattering within itself, and of its music. We find ourselves in Lee Chong's Grocery, on an expedition with marine biologist known as "Doc" (a character based on Steinbeck's friend the marine biologist Ed Ricketts, to whom the book is dedicated) and in the "The Palace Flophouse Bar and Grill." The structure of the book functions much like the introduction and development of the musical themes of an opera, interchanging between vignettes of its perennial people and places and essayistic interludes that attempt to capture the music of the town as a whole. It is in this sense a fitting introduction, or re-introduction, to the music of Steinbeck's literary world, whose themes are often much darker.

2. *To a God Unknown* (1933) (Suggested reading before *East of Eden*)

This slim book took the young Steinbeck five years to write (longer than he spent on either *East of Eden* or *The Grapes of Wrath*). In it, all the essential themes that have their mature expression in *East of Eden* begin to percolate and take form. The farmer's deep, almost familial, relationship to the land he tills is explored--its ups and downs, its great harvests, its too many rains and too few rains. The nature of brotherhood, and the gulfs opened by the differences between brothers, comes to dominate the novel's landscape.

The protagonist, Joseph, bears a name that is never coincidental when attached to stories of brotherhood. The brothers, ona a preacher and one an alcoholic who is murdered early in the story, represent, in a sense, the two opposite ways for sons of farmers to cease to be farmers. Joseph, however, has the deep soul of a farmer, and some of the novel's drama takes place around his brother's theological uneasiness with Joseph's continued conversations with a tree. These archetypal explorations of the relationship between people and the lands and towns they inhabit in Steinbeck's Salinas Valley has for me always hinged on an insight not only into how life can be turned into symbolism, but also on less baroque and more profound insights that symbolism is effective because it resembles life.

3. *In Dubious Battle* (1936) (Suggested Reading before *The Grapes of Wrath*)

This second early novel of Steinbeck's begins to develop the political and social themes that come to dominate his masterpiece *The Grapes of Wrath*, though *In Dubious Battle* is a masterpiece in its own right. Its title taken from Milton's *Paradise Lost*, this novel explores the loss of a different sort of paradise, the loss of a modern utopia, a loss made all the more violent for its genuine clash against the indecencies and unbridled exploitation of mass hunger that California's large scale commercial farmers called the "labor market" of the dustbowl migration.

The book manages a feat rare today and even rarer in the balkanized ideological climate of the early thirties. *In Dubious Battle* eviscerates both the brutality of the system that lead to the immiseration of farmers and comes to discover the boorish opportunism of "The Party." The ACP is never named directly, existing as "The Party" in a royal sense throughout the book in a way that prophetically anticipates both Orwell and the horrors of "really existing communism" for a novel written many decades before the publication of *Gulag Archipelago* and from the perspective of the left. With many gut-wrenching descriptions of the insanity of starvation amidst fields of plenty that presage the most horrifying passages of *Grapes of Wrath*, *In Dubious Battle* also allows us access to the moral sensitivity of Steinbeck. It is a chronicle of the politicization, rise, fall of a single Communist organizer, who becomes a martyr the moment it suits the cynical purpose of his organization. It is a deep meditation on both the necessity and the tragedy of mass political activity that manages to be moral without being moralistic. Finally, it is a work with much to teach us in this era of renewed political anger and demonstrations of all ideological hues.

DANIEL WOODRELL

by Johann Thorsson

I think one of our cardinal fuckups is how we insist that even vicious whimsical crazy shit needs to make sense, add up, belong to a reason. We lay this pain on ourselves--there must be a reason behind this horror, there must, but I ain't adequate to findin' it...

Daniel Woodrell
Tomato Red

Daniel Woodrell (b. 1953) was born in Missouri. He decided he was going to become a writer after trading his lunch for a copy of Hemingway's A Movable Feast on the street in Tijuana. He writes crime fiction, of a sort, that often takes place in the Missouri Ozarks. He found some mainstream success with the movie version of Winter's Bone, but still deserves a larger audience. He won the 1999 PEN USA award for his novel Tomato Red.

It starts like this:

> Jewel Cobb had long been a legendary killer in his midnight reveries and now he'd come to the big town to prove that his upright version knew the same techniques and was just as cold.

That's the first line from the first book in Daniel Woodrell's Bayou Trilogy, and it just gets better from there. I first heard of him around the time that the movie version of *Winter's Bone* was coming out, and after hearing praise from sources I trust, I decided to check the book out. And know this, dear reader, *Winter's Bone* is nothing short of magical. Woodrell rushed into my book-world and was soon crowned king of contemporary writers. This is truly a writer worth your time.

Woodrell writes crime novels, but not of the sort that sit atop bestseller lists. He writes about characters that knowingly get themselves into trouble, drug addicts and small-time crooks. The focus is always on the character.

The writing is always good, and in his later books it becomes downright amazing.

Want to take the Daniel Woodrell trip? Here is my recommendation for how to go about it.

1. *Under the Bright Lights* (1986)

Under the Bright Lights is the first book in Woodrell's Bayou trilogy. These are his most accessible books, since they come very close to the generic "crime is committed, cop with issues investigates" novels that are so popular these days.

The book, and the whole trilogy, focuses on the parish of S. Bruno, the crimes committed by small-time crooks, and the way detective Rene Shade goes about bringing them to justice. The characters in Woodrell's books are deeply flawed, rendered so believably, and, more importantly for us, are so readable. Jewel Cobb, the central character in the book, is such a mess that we can't help but love him, despite the crimes we know he commits. If you read *Under the Bright Lights*, I'm fairly certain you'll read the whole Bayou trilogy.

2. *Give Us A Kiss* (1996)

As with most of his books, Woodrell pulls us right in with the opening line.

*I had a family errand to run, that's all, but I
decided to take a pistol.*

The book then tells us about the trouble Doyle
Redmond, a modestly successful writer, gets into as he
goes in search of his older brother Smoke, who is hiding
out in the Missouri Ozarks. It involves guns, certainly, but
also hillbilly love and past-life experiences. Smoke is
hiding out with two women, Big Annie and Niagra,
whom Doyle promptly falls for. Turns out that Smoke
doesn't much want to go see the law and is in fact
growing quite the crop while in hiding. Doyle finds his
brother just as some local career criminals figure out
about the crop Smoke is growing. Shots get fired.

Give Us a Kiss is different from Woodrell's recent novels
in that the focus is less on the pretty prose (though the
prose *is* all sorts of good) and more on moving the story
along. We are still in familiar territory with unsavory
characters in the Missouri Ozarks up to no good, and we
just can't help but love all the misfits Woodrell drags
onto his pages. There is a point in the book where Doyle
describes how he sees himself as a writer, and this so
mirrors how I imagine Woodrell sees *himself* as a writer
that I felt a pinch of vertigo for a moment, like I was
having an out-of-book experience:

> *I always get called a crime writer, though to me
> they are slice-of-life dramas. They remind me of
> my family and friends, actually. I hate to think I've
> led a 'genre' life, but that seems to be the
> category I'm boxed in.*

3. *Winter's Bone* (2006)

And then there's **Winter's Bone.**

Few books in recent years have reeled me so completely in. I would growl at people disturbing me while I read. I felt cold and hungry the whole time, manifestations of the sympathy I felt for the book's main character, and wanted to reach deep into the Ozarks where the book takes place to give Ree Dolly a hug or food or money. Anything.

The book starts with a police officer showing up at the Dolly residence, a trailer out in the cold woods, and informing sixteen-year-old Ree Dolly that her father has jumped bail, for which he put the house up as insurance. Ree is the oldest of three siblings and is essentially the family matriarch, since her own mother sits in a chair all day, her mind broken from drug use. Ree tries as hard as she can to feed the family and keep the house. The problem is that her father supposedly snitched on local meth dealers and is probably missing for good. But Ree has to find out, has to get proof of his whereabouts or get him to jail again so they won't lose the house. And this puts her in the path of some truly bad people. It wasn't just Ree Dolly that pulled me in, it was also Woodrell's wonderful writing:

> REE DOLLY stood at break of day on her cold front steps and smelled coming flurries and saw meat. Meat hung from trees across the creek. The carcasses hung pale of flesh with a fatty gleam

from low limbs of saplings in the side yards. Three halt haggard houses formed a kneeling rank on the far creekside and each had two or more skinned torsos dangling by rope from sagged limbs, venison left to the weather for two nights and three days so the early blossoming of decay might round the flavor, sweeten that meat to the bone.

The writing is beautiful throughout, stunning really, and I will never tire of recommending this book to people. This is not a feel-good book, none of Mr. Woodrell's books are, but it is good. Perhaps the best book I read in the last few years.

VIRGINIA WOOLF

by Jeanette Solomon

For it would seem - her case proved it - that we write, not with the fingers, but with the whole person. The nerve which controls the pen winds itself about every fibre of our being, threads the heart, pierces the liver.

Virginia Woolf
Orlando

Virginia Woolf *(1882-1941) was one of the most important British modernist writers. Her novels and short stories explored the domestic lives of the British upper-middle class, often from the perspective of women. Using multiple narrators and stream-of-consciousness, Woolf expanded what was possible in English prose.*

Virginia Woolf has the blessing of pop cultural name recognition thanks to Edward Albee's play, *Who's Afraid of Virginia Woolf?* and to Nicole Kidman's Academy Award-winning portrayal of her in *The Hours* (also starring Meryl Streep), adapted from Michael Cunningham's novel of the same name, which drew inspiration from Woolf's own *Mrs. Dalloway*. Of course, in bookish circles, she doesn't need the help of the movies.

Woolf was one of the best-known members of the Bloomsbury Group, a highly influential set of intellectuals whose fingerprints were all over the literature and criticism of the early twentieth century, as well as the modernization of feminism and attitudes toward sexuality. Woolf's own work delves deep into those ideas. Like many writers of her sex, Woolf was keenly aware of women's plight and inequality. She fought against oppression and a society that both implicitly and explicitly hoped to keep women silent, perched on pedestals as a consolation prize. And like so many women writers who railed against these outdated ideas, Woolf committed suicide, filling her coat pockets with stones and walking out into the River Ouse.

For a reader interested in early feminism, I would argue that Woolf is the definitive place to start. (Some will disagree, which is fine. Read what they suggest, too.)

1. "A Room of One's Own" (1929)

An extended essay that explores the notion of women's space in the world, "A Room of One's Own" addresses questions with which women today still must grapple. What is the value of men's space and solitude, as they pore over their studies and create Great Works of Literature? Of women's to do the same? Why is a man's intellectual space prioritized over a woman's?

Here, too, Woolf introduces us to Judith Shakespeare, William's hypothetical sister, to make the point that a woman of William's equal, considerable talent would never have achieved the same level of recognition and staying power because all the doors that were open to him as a man would have remained firmly closed to her. Among many, many other important feminist topics that still stand out today, this one is still my favorite to talk about.

2. *Mrs. Dalloway* (1925)

This innovative, even groundbreaking novel travels in and out of its characters' heads, giving readers an intimate sense of each of them. A day in the life of high-society lady, Mrs. Clarissa Dalloway, as she plans a party is paralleled with that of World War I veteran Septimus Warren Smith, who suffers from "shell shock," what we now know as posttraumatic stress disorder. While Mrs. Dalloway prepares for the party, Mr. Smith commits suicide; she learns of this during her party, and her attitude toward such a controversial act is, to say the least, unconventional. Perhaps, too, it foreshadows Woolf's own death.

3. *Orlando* (1928)

This "biography" is well ahead of its time. It tells the story of Orlando, a man born during the Elizabethan age in England. Stuff happens (I won't give it all away), and one day he wakes up as a woman--still the same person in every other way, but now in a woman's body. The experience is eye-opening, and Orlando decides that being a woman is, overall, superior to being a man. Woolf plays with gender throughout the story, with Orlando alternating between gender roles at pleasure or convenience for the rest of her very long life. Please watch the movie, starring the goddess Tilda Swinton.

After you finish these three, you'll be well prepared to dive into any of Virginia Woolf's other works, and you'll have a few film adaptations to enjoy as well.

CONTRIBUTORS

Benjamin Anders is a writer and graduate student at The New School in New York City.

Tasha Brandstatter is a freelance writer and a regular contributor to History Colorado, the Pueblo PULP, and Opposing Views. She also runs two book blogs: *Truth Beauty Freedom and Books* and *The Project Gutenberg Project*, dedicated to finding forgotten classics.

Josh Corman is a writer and high school English teacher. He lives in Kentucky.

Peter Damien is a writer living in Seattle.

Brenna Clarke Gray holds a PhD in Canadian Literature and teaches in the Vancouver area. She posts about graphic narratives at *Graphixia*, and occasionally on her own blog, *Not That Kind of Doctor*.

Liberty Hardy is a contributing editor at Book Riot and a bookseller at RiverRun Bookstore in Portsmouth, New Hampshire.

Rita Meade lives and works as a public librarian in Brooklyn. She also blogs about her work at I, reviews children's books, and sings in a librarian band.

Loyal Miles is a poet and short story writer living in Brooklyn.

Cassandra Neace is a contributing editor at *Book Riot*.

Jenn Northington has been a bookseller since 2005, has lived all over the United States, and is presently the events manager at WORD in Brooklyn. She also is a founding member of the *Bookrageous* podcast, writes occasionally for Tor.com's "Genre in the Mainstream" series.

Jeff O'Neal is the editor and co-founder of *Book Riot*. He teaches at The New School University in New York City.

Jennifer Paull holds an MA in English Literature from Columbia University and was for many years a travel guidebook editor. She works as an editor for a technology company and lives in Seattle.

Rebecca Joines Schinsky is the senior editor of Book Riot.

Andrew Shaffer is the author of *Literary Rogues*, *Great Philosophers Who Failed at Love*, and, under the pen name Fanny Merkin, *Fifty Shames of Earl Grey: A Parody* (a Goodreads Choice 2012 Semifinalist). His writing has appeared in such diverse publications as *Mental Floss* and *Maxim*.

Jeanette Solomon is a freelance writer with an MA in English Literature.

Kit Steinkellner is a playwright, screenwriter, and creative writing teacher. She also is a contributing editor at *Book Riot* ands writes about books and reading at *Books Are My Boyfriends*.

Johann Thorsson is a writer living in Iceland.

Greg Zimmerman is a contributing editor for *Book Riot*. He blogs about contemporary literary fiction at *The New Dork Review of Books* and holds down a full-time gig as a trade magazine editor.